CAMINO BODYGUARD

a Drew Mallam novel

Mike McBride

For Tom

Buen Camino Peregrino.

Mike

CONTENTS

Title Page	
Prologue: Belfast 1983	1
1. Plymouth, England	11
2. Logroño to Nájera	21
3. Nájera	34
4. Nájera to Santo Domingo	43
5. Santo Domingo de la Calzada	54
6. Santo Domingo to Castildelgardo	66
7. Castildelgardo to Belorado	71
8. Belorado	86
9. Belorado to San Juan	93
10. San Juan de Ortega	101
11. San Juan to Burgos	107
12. Burgos	117
13. Burgos to Hornillos	131
14. Hornillos del Camino	137
15. Hornillos to Castrojeriz	148

16. Castrojeriz	156
17. Castrojeriz to Frómista	166
18. Frómista	172
19. Frómista to Carrión	178
20. Carrión de los Condes	190
21. Carrión to Terradillos	201
22. Terradillos de la Templarios	207
23. Terradillos to Sahagún	217
24. Sahagún	221
25. Sahagún to El Burgo Ranero	236
Epilogue: Lavacolla to Santiago	245
Camino Veteran Prologue: Moscow & Paris	251
Camino Veteran	255
Acknowledgements	256
Copyright © Mike McBride, 2024	257
Books by this Author	258

PROLOGUE: BELFAST 1983

Death was swift. The full metal jacket bullet entered the left side of the neck bisecting the carotid and jugular blood vessels, as well as the vagus nerve. The bullet struck the cervical vertebrae. Already the catastrophic damage caused to the body was incompatible with human life.

The impact against the vertebrae severed the spinal cord and the bullet lost its integrity. Multiple sharp copper fragments deflected, inflicting massive tissue damage.

Mercifully, it was unlikely that they felt anything in the milliseconds it took for the bullet to wreak havoc.

One minute before this happened, a young soldier was treading cautiously along an alleyway, next to a derelict house on the main street. It had started to rain. 'Welcome to Ulster's eleven month rainy season,' he muttered to himself.

He looked around to check his section commander, Corporal Dickinson, was still there. Behind the Corporal was a young RUC policewoman, followed by Fusilier Smith carrying the electronic jamming manpack and behind him the new guy, Fusilier Lane, as tailend Charlie.

Using his left hand, as if he was bowling an invisible cricket ball underarm, the Corporal urged the first Fusilier forward. In a London accent he whispered, "Get a fakin' move on."

The patrol had already taken too long escorting the policewoman around her beat. Several snotty kids had given them aggro and lobbed a few bricks. The Corporal carried a 37 mm riot gun and had threatened the ringleader with a baton round in the balls if he did not piss off. That did the trick, he thought. Some people only react to force. It had started to rain. Sod it.

The lead Fusilier took a quick look left and right along the street. Thankfully all quiet. No young toughs wanting to hurl abuse or have a scrap. Just a few parked cars and a tipper truck about 200 metres down the street to the left. He gave a thumbs up sign and darted around the corner to the left and took up a covering position in the front door of the boarded-up house. Something felt wrong. The Fusilier's senses were tingling. It was far too quiet. The street was deserted.

In an upstairs front bedroom of a house, halfway between the alleyway and the tipper truck, a video camera was recording.

The Corporal took up a position on the corner of the alleyway and scanned the empty wet street. From behind him, Fusilier Smith bellowed, "Watch out! Remote signal detected. Take cov-."

An earth-shattering explosion rent the air as a massive improvised bomb detonated inside the derelict house. A flash of flame shot out and the front of the house blew into the street, like the world's biggest blunderbuss. As bricks, slates, timbers and glass flew forwards the upper storey and roof fell down causing a huge cloud of smoke and dust. Debris from the house formed a shoulder-high pile across the pavement between the first Fusilier and his Corporal.

The Corporal was dazed and deafened by the blast. Smoke was blinding his eyes. A smell like fireworks filled his nostrils. Car alarms sounded, glass fragments crashed down and it rained debris.

A crack-thump was followed by another. Now they were being shot at. The first sound was made by the bullet flying past at supersonic speed; the second was the blast from the muzzle of the rifle which was travelling at the speed of sound. The explosion and the shooting simply overwhelmed the Corporal's senses.

"They're shooting at *yer* man!" screamed the policewoman into the Corporal's ear. "A gunman is firing at *yer* leading soldier!"

Fear gripped the Corporal.

"Do something Corporal. They're going to kill him. For the love of God, help him!" the policewoman begged.

From behind the pile of rubble, the policewoman could just make out muzzle flashes from the tipper truck. A gunman was firing blindly into the cloud of smoke and dust that used to be a house. The lead Fusilier lay face down on the pavement. Although partially covered by bricks, he was totally exposed to the gunfire from the shooter in the truck.

The Corporal stayed behind the debris, motionless.

Gallantly, the policewoman ran through the dust cloud to the downed Fusilier, grabbed the shoulders of his flak jacket and tried to drag him into cover. Crack-thump. The gunman's view was improving as the dust was settling. Crack-thump. Crack-thump.

Bit by bit, the policewoman started to move the unconscious Fusilier to safety. His rifle was still attached to his wrist by its sling, it clattered along behind them.

The policewoman dragged the soldier along agonisingly slowly. Each time the gunman fired it energised her to superhuman effort. Crack-thump.

The gunman's shots were becoming more accurate. The rounds were landing closer and closer. Crack-thump.

The policewoman had almost got the soldier behind the pile of debris and made one last heave, when a thousand-to-one shot caught the officer in the neck. Thud-thump.

The Corporal saw the policewoman get shot and collapse, immediately falling backwards onto him. There was very little blood from the neck wound and from the odd angle of the officer's head, it looked like her neck was broken as well. He was certain she was dead.

Fusilier Smith came from the debris strewn alleyway, "What the effs 'appening Dixie?"

It was like a switch had been flipped and seeing the policewoman die right in front of him made the Corporal snap into action. He pushed her off him and pressed transmit on his radio, "Contact! Contact! Wait out."

The radio responded, "Unknown callsign. Say again. Over."

"Smudger, we've been fired at from a truck down the street. It's just fackin' driven off now," Corporal Dickinson took a breath. His next utterance was a life changer, "I dragged Mallam back here and am shoutin' to the woman Peeler here to keep her 'ed down. Just as I get into cover, doesn't she take a look over the pile of rubble? She cops a round in the neck. Brown bread. Poor gal. Mallam here is knocked out and has multiple injuries." Then the Corporal shouted, "What a crap day!"

The radio channel came alive with multiple

transmissions. Units shouting that they had heard an explosion, others reporting the sound of gunshots. And all demanding more information.

Major Hudson was universally liked by those in C Company, but nobody dared interrupt him on the radio, as his temper at having to repeat what he had just said was as legendary as his stutter, "Unknown callsign this is Sunray. Say again your contact st... st... status. Over."

Corporal Dickinson transmitted as calmly as he could, "Zero, this is India Three Six Charlie. Contact. Dover Street. Command detonation of derelict building. Follow up attack from a gunman in the rear of a truck. Truck has now made off in the direction of Victoria Hospital. Roger so far?"

Major Hudson replied, "R... R... Roger so far. Out to you. Hello Tango One One, dispatch QRF towards Dover Street. Approach with caution. Possible sec... sec... secondary explosive device waiting for you. Over."

"Tango One One. Roger out," said the clipped public school tones of the quick reaction force subaltern.

"This is Sunray. All ca... ca... callsigns minimise on this channel. India Three Six Charlie what is your casualty status over?" said Major Hudson.

"India Three Six Charlie," said the Corporal, "one Greenfinch KIA with GSW to her head. One Fusilier unconscious with multiple blast injuries. Request casevac. Over." Corporal Dickinson's training had finally kicked in. He was mentally working through his 'actions on', the standard operating procedures for a terrorist attack. Reporting that a policewoman had been killed and one of their own men blown up would cause stress levels to increase exponentially right across the battalion's radio network.

The QRF subaltern took up position in the turret of the first of four Saracen armoured personnel carriers. The six wheeled Saracens' Rolls-Royce engines were already ticking over. Each vehicle contained a commander, driver and six soldiers.

To the control room the subaltern radioed calmly, "Tango One One, en route to Dover Street. Out." To his driver he switched to the intercom, "Okay. Driver advance." To the soldiers at the gates he shouted, "Get those bloody gates open!" The engines of the four Saracens screamed as they raced towards the incident.

The cameraman heard the Saracens approach before he saw them nose into Dover Street. Time to go. He switched off the camera, packed it all away and scurried out of the backdoor and away down a maze of alleyways.

The QRF cordoned off the street. The subaltern spoke to Corporal Dickinson, who was waiting for an ambulance with the now conscious Fusilier Mallam, "What the hell happened here Corporal?" demanded the young officer.

"Sir, we were on an escort patrol for the RUC. We took a bit of low-level aggro from some young bucks, then we came down the alley to Dover Street. It looked okay, so we moved on and Fusilier Smith heard a remote control detonation signal through the jammer. The signal was a new one which we haven't jammed before. He shouted for us to take cover and the building just blew up.

"Then a gunman in the back of a parked tipper truck started firing at us. I think it was an Armalite," He paused, then repeated the awful lie, "Fusilier Mallam was unconscious and injured, so I had to run out from cover and drag him back. I shouted to the Greenfinch to stay down in cover, but she looked up and was hit in the neck. Died instantly. Nothing we could do boss. I couldn't return fire at the tipper truck as the hospital was the backstop. The truck drove off."

The subaltern saw that a green poncho had been draped over the dead policewoman next to the wounded Fusilier Mallam, who was waiting for casualty evacuation. The officer went off to ensure his troop sergeant had deployed the soldiers to his particular liking.

"Dixie, I heard what you said to the officer," croaked Fusilier Mallam, coughing brick dust from his throat.

"Just rest now, me old china. You need to

conserve your strength for those nurses back at Musgrave military hospital you lucky bastard," he said trying to reassure his wounded comrade with a bit of humour.

"I will never forget what you did for me, you crazy heroic cockney tosser," the Fusilier said, through gritted teeth as another wave of searing pain from his left arm and leg hit him.

"Put a sock in it. I couldn't leave you out there like a figure eleven target to get pumped full of 'oles." Thinking that an opportunity might just emerge from this tragedy.

"I mean it. I owe you one. If ever you need my help. Ever. Just ask Dixie. Okay?"

A few months later in the London Evening Standard there was an article:

Royal Recognition for Cockney Hero.
East End boy defies sniper to save buddy in IRA ambush.
Sergeant Peter Dickinson, 29, originally from Mile End Road, saved Fusilier Andrew Mallam from almost certain death in a fiendish bomb and sniper ambush in Belfast last year. Details have only recently emerged of the heroic actions of the cockney soldier when he was awarded the British Empire Medal by Her Majesty the Queen, at Buckingham Palace last week.
Sergeant Dickinson was a Corporal at the time when he led a four-man patrol to escort a Royal Ulster Constabulary policewoman around her beat, to bring back a sense of normality to the troubled province, when the PIRA struck. Firstly, the terrorists detonated a huge bomb in a derelict

house they were passing. Fusilier Mallam was knocked out and was being shot at by a sniper. The medal citation reads, 'Without hesitation Corporal Dickinson ran forwards to drag a wounded soldier to safety under heavy and sustained small arms fire, undoubtedly saving his comrade from death or serious injury. His actions are in the highest traditions of the regiment...'

The Commanding Officer, Lieutenant-Colonel Charles Hudson commented, 'Sergeant Dickinson is a professional soldier through and through. Utterly fearless.'

In a sad twist to this incident the RUC policewoman died at the scene due to a gunshot wound.

Shortly after the incident, in a smoke-filled back room, the PIRA Army Council watched the video. Due to poor grade nitrogen fertiliser only half of the bomb in the building actually detonated, the marksmanship of their volunteer was woeful and instead of elimination of the soldiers of the British state they killed a brave young Irish woman, in an RUC uniform. They unanimously decided to have the video tape destroyed.

Unknown to the army council the cameraman had made a copy of the video.

1. PLYMOUTH, ENGLAND

Drew Mallam's phone rang. It was an unknown number. Nope, not today, he thought and hung up. A minute later a message alert came through. Intrigued, Drew accessed his voicemail inbox. There was one new message. He pressed play. His life would never be the same again.

"Hello, me old china. Do you know who this is? Blast from the past. Excuse the pun. It's your old mucker Dixie. Would like to have a bit of a catch-up. Please call me back as soon as convenient. Like now! (laughs)."

Drew hadn't heard from Peter Dickinson, Dixie, in years. After he left the Army, Dixie was in great demand as a close protection expert and security consultant to the rich and famous. Still dining out on stories of derring-do from back in the day.

No time like the present Drew thought, so he rang back. His call was answered before the second ring, "Hey Drew! Thanks for calling me back. How are you?" The years since Drew and Dixie served in the same regiment evaporated, they spoke as if it was yesterday.

"I'm very well. Living in obscurity. Retired and happy. More importantly, how are you?" Drew asked.

"Living the dream. I call myself the Security Czar, for a multi-billion dollar company headquartered in Johannesburg. In reality, I feel like a minor functionary. Mr Dogsbody. Ha ha," Peter said, cheerfully.

"Anyway, what can I do for you Dixie?"

"Well I need to pick your brains. Delicate subject, so face-to-face would be best. Are you free to meet-up?" asked Peter.

"Well that depends. I take it that you know I live in Plymouth, I'm not likely to be in Joburg anytime soon," Drew was not prepared for what Peter was to say next.

"That's okay. As it 'appens I'm in Plymouth right now. Can we meet today? Or better still... today? I'm staying down in the Barbican, so suggest an RV. Somewhere discreet."

"Er... okay. The Minerva pub in Looe Street might be suitable for us. How about one o'clock?" Drew said, puzzled.

"Sounds great. I will find it and see you there matey. Thirteen hundred hours, sharp."

"Ahoy there! Is that what you say down here Drew?" said Peter, offering his old comrade a firm handshake, as they met in the Minerva Inn.

"Not unless you're a matelot. Good to see you. What the hell are you doing in Plymouth, Dixie?"

asked Drew.

"Would you believe it, I'm just here to see you matey? I have business to sort out in London, but have come down to ask if you can help me out with something. That's all," he lied. "Pint is it?"

"No thanks. I think I will have a tonic and ice to keep a clear head with you. You do know I'm retired?" Drew said, more than a little confused.

"I know. Alright, I know. Don't be all defensive. How many times have I got you out of sticky situations when we were back in the regiment? That's before you buggered off to do bomb disposal. Quite funny in an ironic way. Anyway, it's good to see you after all this time. You're looking fit," said Peter, noticing that Drew was still in reasonable shape, for a retired old soldier.

"Thanks. You're looking-"

"Well nourished?" Peter interrupted.

"I was going to say 'prosperous,'" said Drew, chuckling.

"I was surprised to find out that you'd ended up down here in Plymouth. I thought you were a northern lad," said Peter, paying the barmaid for the drinks with a platinum company credit card.

"Well what can I say? I just can't get enough of clotted cream teas."

"I can never remember in Devon. Is it cream on the scone first, or is it the jam?" asked Peter.

"Unless you want to start a fight, my advice is just don't go there," said Drew, shaking his head.

Drew and Peter took their drinks to a table at

the back of the pub, so they could talk in peace.

"So, cards on the table, I need a bit of help," said Peter, in a low tone.

"You do remember me just telling you that I'm retired?"

"I know. Just hear me out, matey. I work for Paul de Witt. His company supplies industrial and farming equipment throughout Africa, and beyond in fact. Anyway, they make most of their money not on new sales, but on maintenance and training. It's a massive company. Good people. Really good people," said Peter, taking a long swig of beer.

"Okay. Go on," said Drew, cautiously.

"Well, Paul is in his late seventies and is thinking of succession planning," Peter used air quotation marks when he said the words, 'succession planning.'

"He has just one son, John, who is twenty. Here's the rub. John was abducted last year in the Caribbean for about a week, ransom paid out, police hostage rescue went in and the three gang members got shot dead by the SWAT team. Did you hear about it?" Peter asked, with a knowing grin.

"Can't say that I did," Drew said, slightly confused.

Peter's smile broadened, "That's 'cos it was all hushed up. Like it never 'appened. Still a few loose ends to the kidnapping. Firstly, how did the kidnappers know to target John? Then, where did all the money go? And, was there a fourth member of the gang masterminding it all?"

"How much ransom was involved?" asked Drew, sipping his tonic.

"Oh it was the usual rubbish. The kidnappers always ask for ten million US and settle for a fraction of it. It was two and half million we agreed to pay. It was going great. Sweet as a nut, you could say. The handover of John was all arranged."

"What could possibly go wrong?" said Drew, sensing that something awful did.

"Then, the night before the handover, the police got a tip-off and went all Robocop on the gang. Shot the bloomin' lot of them. I can't blame the police. They want to eliminate the crime gangs, but now we'll never know if anyone else was involved."

"Where did the money go?" asked Drew, still trying to figure out what all this had to do with him.

"The board asked me that too," said Peter, raising his eyebrows as if he had been asked the same old question multiple times. "I told them that the important thing was to get John back. That was the first priority. The money was transferred electronically and went down a rabbit hole from one bogus account to another in milliseconds. It's gone. Insurance has paid out. End of, as far as I'm concerned."

"Very interesting as all this is Dixie, I'm at a loss about what help you're after."

"Alright you narky old sod, keep your hair on,

what's left of it. Right, so John is all shook up about being kidnapped. Being threatened with having his balls cut off, then the rescue when the gang members are all brassed up by the cops around him. Kind of upset the young lad," said Peter, laconically.

"Yes, I imagine it would irk him a bit," noted Drew, flatly.

"So, for a year he has been on an almighty bender. Drink, drugs, the whole shebang. Thing is he needs rehabilitation, but he says 'No. No. No!'"

"How very Amy Winehouse."

"Indeed matey. Well instead of a stay in a clinic, he's become obsessed with walking that pilgrimage route you've done," said Peter.

It was now starting to make some sense to Drew. Peter must have found out on the grapevine that Drew had already been on several pilgrimages since retiring. "The *Camino de Santiago*? That's easy, there's loads of information online. He doesn't need me to advise him," said Drew, emphatically.

Dixie looked Drew in the eye, "Not to advise him matey. To go with him."

Drew reflected on this. Ah! So this is what it's all about, he thought to himself. He was being asked to look after a traumatised, alcoholic, drug addict, an ultra-high- net-worth VIP and a kidnap risk - on a pilgrimage.

"The answer is a hard 'no,'" said Drew, "but I'm a bit puzzled. Why me?"

Undaunted, Peter continued, "It's a question of trust. Paul and John both trust me. And I trust you. Simple as that.

"Also, we can't send in a close protection team to bodyguard John conventionally on the pilgrimage. It would just cause more problems. Can you imagine a squad of former special forces operatives in a box formation around him, all cheap suits and sunglasses, talking up their cuffs into microphones?" laughed Peter.

"I suppose not," said Drew, realising Peter's predicament.

"It has to be low key. Just someone providing him with what I'd call 'protective surveillance.' Keeping an eye on the lad. That's all. John is a good kid. I've known him since he was in primary school."

"I'm sorry you've wasted your time coming down here, but it's still a big fat 'no.'" said Drew, firmly.

There was a long pause. Peter took another gulp of beer and thought through his next sentence with care.

"I didn't want to do this to you Andrew... but I remember a badly wounded soldier lying in the rubble on a rain-soaked Belfast street saying that if I ever needed help then he would be there for me. Now I need your help matey. I'm calling in the promise you made to me."

Drew paused, looked down, then whispered, "You bastard."

After a painfully long silence Drew said, "Okay, so if I'm going to do this thing. And it's still a big if, brief me up."

"Time is short. John needs to be clean for at least a month before his twenty-first birthday in December for him to qualify for his trust fund. If he's not clean he misses out on a few quid."

"By a 'few quid' you mean a few million?" ventured Drew.

Peter smiled and ignored the question, "You will get a prepaid *euro* currency card for all expenses incurred and to access cash from ATMs."

"I presume you will need receipts for everything," said Drew.

"Nope. You're in the Circle of Trust, me old china," Peter said cheerfully. "I will monitor expenditure and keep the card topped up to at least a thousand *euros.* Plus at the end of the contract you will receive a consultancy fee of a thousand pounds per day, or part thereof."

Drew thought for a few seconds, "Okay. Issue one is I don't want a few thou dropping into my bank account. I could get clobbered for tax."

"Does cash work for you?" asked Peter.

"Er... cash, could work. Secondly, I'm not going to be beholden to any *Camino* contract. I'm retired, remember."

"Mmm, that might be an issue with our bean counters. They do like everyone to be tucked up with contracts, non-disclosures and all that kind of crap. Okay, let's call it a 'gentleman's agreement' and we will seal it with a handshake," said Peter.

"Well actually, I was planning on walking another section of the *Camino Frances* anyway in a week or two. I'll do it. But after this Dixie the favour is repaid, in full. Got it?"

"I saved yer bleedin' life. You could be a bit more soddin' grateful," said Peter, with mock exasperation.

"What would my duties be?" asked Drew.

"Meet me and John at a place of your choosing. Walk with him. Mentor him on *Camino* etiquette. Advise him to refrain from drink and drugs. Assess risks. Report to me daily. There will be an exfiltration plan in case his identity is compromised and things go tits-up."

"Surely his passport will be a bit of a give away," said Drew.

"Actually he travels as John Derwent and he has been drilled as to his cover story."

"Will you quartermaster his kit?" asked Drew.

"Yeah of course. What does he need?" asked Peter, making notes on his phone.

"Check online to see what pilgrims recommend, but keep his pack weight to six kilos, or less. Oh, and make sure he comes with well worn footwear."

Other administrative details were discussed before they both stood up and shook hands.

"So Drew, what are you doing this afternoon?" asked Peter.

"Looks like I will be packing my rucksack and I

can feel a ferry booking to Spain coming on. What about you?" asked Drew.

"Got a couple of hours before my train back to London so I thought I'd have a little look at HMS Victory while I'm here."

"You must have bloody good eyesight. The last time I heard, Victory was still in Portsmouth you plonker," said Drew, laughing.

"Oh bugger," said Peter. "'Ere did you know that this pub was a famous haunt of the Press Gang?"

"It bloody well still is," replied Drew, with a wry smile.

2. LOGROÑO TO NÁJERA

<u>606 km to Santiago de Compostela.</u>

A sixty-something man in hiking clothes and a rucksack entered the reception area at the hotel Áurea Palacio de Correos in Logroño.

Peter Dickinson approached the pilgrim with a worried expression on his face. Drew said, "Wassup, Dixie?" shaking hands with his old comrade.

"There's been a hiccup in the giddyup, you could say," replied Peter, glumly.

"You mean some sort of a cockup?"

"Yes. Little Lord Fauntleroy had, let's say, a 'crisis of confidence' last night. So he hit the minibar," explained Peter.

"Do you mean John drank the overpriced sparkling water and scoffed the bar of chocolate?"

"And the beers, the wines, then all of the miniatures," Peter said, grimacing, "before finishing his evening off by nipping out for a bottle of bourbon as a nightcap."

"Is he still alive?" asked Drew, incredulously.

"Well, what's left of him is in a very sorry state matey. He was calling for Huey down the big white telephone all night. Let's go sort out the little lad and give him a quiet word shall we?" said Peter, as he headed towards the lift.

They entered John de Witt's bedroom and a pathetic muffled voice from under the bedding moaned, "Pete, I'm taking a duvet day. Start first thing tomorrow."

"That's not how it's going to be John," responded Peter cheerily. "The sun's burning, the world's turning, it's time for you to hit the road. Get a wash, you'll feel better."

In one swift action Peter dragged the bedding off John who adopted the foetal position, hugging his pillow for comfort. Thankfully a pair of boxer shorts spared everyone's embarrassment.

Drew would describe John as having the physique of a surfer who had 'let himself go' a bit. Lanky suntanned limbs, flabby stomach and long unkempt hair. With some sort of antelope tattoo on his upper right arm.

Reluctantly, John got up and pushed a mop of unruly blonde hair out of his eyes. He stumbled into the bathroom making little pained noises, "Pete, you're a proper bastard you know. *Ag* man! Andrew shouldn't see me like this," he whined.

"A bastard is usually someone just doing their job," said Peter, without emotion.

Once John had shuffled into the bathroom, Peter picked up a half full bottle of bourbon from the floor. "At least he didn't finish it," he said, thankfully.

Drew opened John's rucksack and tipped the contents out onto the bed. Item by item he went through the stuff, only repacking the bare necessities. Peter scooped up a heap of excess kit and stuffed it into a large holdall.

A few minutes later, John came back into the room and got dressed into his hiking clothes.

"You won't be needing that," said Drew, throwing a South African Springboks cap into the holdall. "We will get you something better on the way."

"A journey of a thousand miles starts with a single step, said some clever sod," Peter announced, as he invited John to follow Drew out of the hotel room and towards reception.

Drew and John walked to the hotel front door, as Peter called out breezily, "Missing you already boys. Do keep in touch." He smiled and raised his hand to his ear, as if he was holding a phone.

Down the street Drew popped into a souvenir shop. He emerged with a beige baseball cap with a yellow arrow motif on the front.

He put it on John's head, "Marvellous! Keep it on as much as you can. It's amazing how lots of celebs go unnoticed by just wearing a cap."

"I'd prefer my Springboks cap," said John,

grumpily.

"Let's make people work to get information about you," said Drew as he scanned the pavement for a brass *Camino* marker.

"Are you lost already?" said John, smirking.

"Not yet. Just following the markers. You'll know when I'm lost, I will ask you to show me where we are on your mapping app."

"How far are we going today?" asked John, in a crotchety tone.

Drew thought, if John starts asking, Are we there yet? every five minutes, I might have a sense-of-humour-failure. What he actually said was, "Nájera, it's about twenty-eight kilometres. And I've taken the liberty of booking us into a modest hotel. No hostel for us tonight."

John grunted. Drew gritted his teeth and mentally counted to ten.

Drew had a lot on his mind. On previous *Caminos*, he only had to worry about himself. How he would get from A to B. What route would he take? When would he get there? Where would he stop? What was he going to eat? Life was simple back then. Now, he had John de Witt to consider. Things had not got off to a good start.

They were nearing the edge of town and walking through parklands. The brass markers inlaid into the pavement had given way to official blue and yellow signs, as well as unofficial yellow arrows spray painted on street furniture or on the path itself.

"It's obvious why I'm on the *Camino*, but I haven't figured out why you are," said John, trying to start a conversation to distract himself from the ordeal of walking with a colossal hangover.

"Okay I'll bite. Why are you on it?" asked Drew.

"If I don't detox, I'm a dead man. You hear about so many celebrities who isolate themselves with a gang of cronies filling their head with nonsense, when they could be out here actually feeling something. The fresh air and the exercise is better than overdosing in a soulless mansion," John spoke with real conviction.

"So this is your 'last chance saloon?'" asked Drew.

"Poor choice of words to a recovering alcoholic, but *ja*."

From Drew's first impression of John, he was far more of the 'alcoholic' and precious little of the 'recovering'. "Nothing to do with being clean on your twenty-first birthday to qualify for a trust fund then?"

"*Ag.* What's the use of all that money if I'm dead, eh? It can be a curse ya know," John sounded thoughtful, then tried to get back to his original line, "but hey, don't dodge the question, Andrew. Why are you doing this bodyguard contract? Just the money? A hired gunslinger?"

"Ha! Firstly, I'm not a bodyguard. I'm just here

to guide you. Keep an eye out for you is all. And for your information there is no *Camino* contract," said Drew, "and, sorry to disappoint you still further - no gun either."

"Really? Nobody works for us unless they're tucked up with a watertight contract. And I can't believe you're not armed. You do know I was kidnapped?" John said, incredulously.

Drew explained that he did not work for John, his family or the business. It was simply a gentleman's agreement with Peter Dickinson.

"What? You're not being paid? Ah! I see. Pete is blackmailing you. What does he have over you to make you be my nanny, eh?"

"Think I will leave you guessing on that one John. One thing that does appeal to me is the thought that I can help you get clean. If you are committed to face your demons and keep off the booze and drugs, then I'm prepared to help you."

"You're like the Good Samaritan, Andrew. It must have been a shock to find out I got hammered last night then."

"I will admit, it was a surprise,' said Drew, 'and if you pull a stunt like that again, you're on your own, John."

"You can't," said John, defiantly.

Drew smiled and simply shook his head.

The Way continued through formal parkland

into the countryside. The pair were kept busy acknowledging, "*Buen Camino,*" greetings from the passing walkers, runners and the occasional cyclist.

"Ah. Dutchman's trousers. Good!" said Drew, looking up at the cloudy sky.

"What utter word salad are you spouting there, *Ouballie*?" said John addressing Drew in *Afrikaaner* slang for 'old man', as he adjusted the shoulder straps on his rucksack.

"Sailors used to say that if you can see at least two bits of blue sky, enough to patch a Dutchman's trousers, it won't rain."

"Let's see," said John, doubtfully.

As they skirted the reservoir outside Logroño they saw a mobile coffee stall set up in a woodland clearing.

"Fancy a coffee, John?" said Drew, happily.

John looked up from the trail and nodded, he could do with a rest. They put their rucksacks down on the benches.

Drew established that John preferred a large coffee with lots of hot milk, which happened to be the ever-popular pilgrims' choice - *café con leche grande*. Drew got himself a *cortado*, which had a double hit of coffee and not so much milk.

"Hey, I suppose I should thank you for putting all my extra stuff into the holdall. My rucksack is heavy enough," said John, rubbing his shoulders.

"Ah, it's not a problem."

"The holdall will be waiting at the hotel

tonight I'm guessing," said John.

Drew appeared to be looking up for inspiration and said, "How to manage your expectations? Hmm. Nope."

"*Ag*! I need that stuff, man," whined John.

"You want that stuff," said Drew, with special emphasis on 'want.' "You'll be fine with less. The holdall will be waiting at *Casa Ivar* in Santiago for you to pick it up when you get there."

"*Ag* man. You mean if I get there," John was finding the walking monotonous, his rucksack was digging into his shoulders and his feet were sore. The feeling of rapture, experienced by some pilgrims, had thus far eluded him. He was hungover, tired, tetchy and twenty.

They finished their coffees and strapped on their rucksacks, "Let's walk," said Drew and he set off with John following a few metres behind like a sullen child.

The clouds had broken up. There was a light breeze and it had become pleasantly warm. Ideal walking weather.

Drew was happy to see plenty of red squirrels. They were practically extinct where he lived in Devon. Ousted by the ubiquitous grey squirrel, a bigger sub-species and much better at being a squirrel than their red cousins. He wanted to discuss his theory with John that a squirrel was little more than a rat with a good PR firm, but John looked like the picture of abject unhappiness. They continued walking along in silence.

Halfway between Navarrette and Ventosa, a picnic area had been built next to a factory. Drew looked at his watch. It was approaching midday, time for a break.

"Lunchtime, John," said Drew. They had not uttered a word to each other for more than an hour. The silence had become deafening.

"Great! I'm starving. I've had no breakfast," John replied, looking around for whatever restaurant Drew had in mind.

Drew unclipped his straps, before slipping off his rucksack and putting it on the stone table.

"Ideally, what would you like for your lunch?" asked Drew.

"Ah, an aged Aberdeen Angus T-bone steak, cooked rare," said John, hopefully, "with a decent red wine sauce, grilled Portobello garlic mushrooms and loads of triple cooked chips."

Drew opened his rucksack and took a long look inside his food bag, "Would you settle for half a cheese and *jamón baguette*, with a boiled egg?"

"Sounds *lekker*," said John, derisively.

John dropped his pack onto a rotted tree stump. Drew winced, "You may wish to put your rucksack on the table."

Drew explained that bed bugs thrived in rotting wood and caught a ride into their eponymous homes in *albergues* on the base of rucksacks. Which was why seasoned pilgrims never put their backpacks on their mattresses.

Drew used a hand sanitizer before giving it to John, then he passed him a *baguette*, slightly crushed, wishing him, "*Bon appetit.*"

They ate in silence and afterwards Drew swapped his socks for a fresh pair.

"Okay. Now you John. Boots off and change your socks," said Drew.

"Oh it's okay. I don't need to right now," said John absentmindedly, whilst engrossed on his phone.

John then received a lecture on basic foot care from Drew and wisely decided to put on a fresh pair of socks. They slipped on their rucksacks. "Let's walk," said Drew.

After a while Drew said, "Some people find a *Camino* a great opportunity to have a data-fast John."

"Ah huh," said John, looking at his phone as he tramped along.

Another minute went by, "Yes, they find it allows them to be 'in the moment' if you know what that means?"

"Suppose so," said John, still scrolling through

his social media accounts and hoping Drew would shut up soon.

Shortly afterwards Drew said, "Yes, you know they like mindfulness. The luxury of switching off their tech, you know?"

John stopped. "You are talking verbal diarrhoea man, *praatsiek* we call it. What are you trying to say?" He was now thoroughly irritated by Drew.

Drew looked at John, "Turn that bloody phone off."

John hesitated, but felt slightly threatened by Drew's tone. He switched off his phone, "Happy now?" he said, bitterly.

"Ah, that's much better," said Drew, grinning like the Cheshire cat.

"It's not fair. You'll be begging me to switch it back on when you get lost," muttered John.

"When 'we' get lost," said Drew, still smiling and enjoying the little victory. God this is going to be a long walk, thought Drew. So did John.

September was a busy time of year on the *Camino Frances*. Already Drew and John had met other pilgrims including a lawyer from London, a semi-retired carpenter from Sweden, and a retired chemist from Seattle. Drew handled the interactions between the other pilgrims. John would have said 'dominated' the interactions, as if to always sideline him.

"How are you going to handle questions from other pilgrims about yourself?" asked Drew, when they were walking on a stretch on their own.

"I've got my cover story sorted," said John.

"Good. Try and be as uninteresting as you can."

"Pete said I should be the 'Grey Man.'"

"Exactly right. If you were in a crowd, you wouldn't stand out. People looking at a group would look at you, then keep on scanning. Peter has taught you well," said Drew.

"So I guess you owe Pete a favour," John said, trying to irritate Drew.

Silence.

Drew smiled and thought to himself, you can keep on knocking on my door John all day long, but I'm not answering.

After a long silence. "Yep. A big favour I reckon... Really big," said John.

More deafening silence. What you don't realise John, is I've done Resistance to Interrogation training in the military. You're getting f-all from me, and plenty of it, thought Drew, confidently.

"More than just something like money," John said, looking sideways at Drew to see if he could tell anything from his facial expression. "What's more important than money? Mmm, some other debt you owe him... Your life! Yes, he saved your life. When you were soldiers. Is that it? Is it? Is that the reason you're helping Pete?" said John, happy in his mind that he had established Drew's true motivation.

Drew just rolled his eyes and shook his head.

"Yeah. I'm right! I'm damned right," shouted John, with a satisfied grin.

◆ ◆ ◆

Drew had taken off his windcheater top. The breeze and midday sun had made the walking agreeable, even if the atmosphere between the pair was anything but.

They decided to bypass Ventosa, and its charms, in favour of the direct approach into Nájera.

September also brought in the season of mellow fruitfulness and the opportunity to do a bit of foraging on The Way. The blackberries were in season. Sweet and tasty, but a little smaller and less juicy than the ones back in England. The red grapes, in the massive vineyards, were also super sweet, almost ready for harvesting. The olives were not yet ripe. Tasting an olive straight from the tree would leave a bitter taste in the mouth, not quickly forgotten. The figs were plentiful and would no doubt nourish pilgrims in October, when they were ready.

Eventually, Nájera came into sight. Which was a relief for both men.

3. NÁJERA

When the pilgrims reached Nájera, Drew stopped at an ATM and withdrew some cash, using the travel money card Peter had given him. They went into a *supermercado* and Drew bought some snacks, apples, bread and sliced cheese. In the shop, John picked up a large glass jar of hazelnut chocolate spread.

"Are you happy to carry that?" asked Drew.

John hefted the weighty jar in his hand, sighed and put it back on the shelf.

Hostal Hispano was simple to find. Straight into Nájera, turn left before the river and it was on the left.

"I thought you said we weren't staying in a hostel tonight?" said John, a little confused by the sign Hostal Hispano. Drew explained that a hostel offered dormitory accommodation; whereas, a hostal was a no-frills hotel.

As Drew checked in with the receptionist, he found that she would machine-wash their clothes. He paid upfront for the two rooms and the laundry service in cash.

"Why does climbing stairs feel so tough, man?" complained John, as they walked up to the first floor.

"Just one of the many gifts the *Camino* is bestowing on you," said Drew, in a cheery way calculated to annoy his exhausted companion. When they reached the landing, they found their doorway which led to two separate bedrooms, with a shared bathroom. Drew inspected both rooms and invited John to choose the one he wanted.

"Hey, what are all those big bags and packs with labels doing on the landing?" asked John.

"Oh yes. I'd say they are for pilgrims using the baggage transport service," said Drew.

"So, you mean they're cheating?"

Drew laughed, "I wouldn't say so. I mean if I pick up an injury and have to decide to either quit the *Camino* or have *Correos* transport my load - then that's fine by me."

John was confused, "Who's this Corry Oz dude?"

"The *Correos* is the postal service here in Spain. They operate the baggage transfer, as do other companies. It's quite a slick operation, so I'm led to believe. There is an app and all.

"Righto, it's shower time, then sort out anything you need washing and I'll take it to the receptionist. Do you want to use the bathroom first?"

John decided that catching up on his phone took priority over showering.

Drew spread the minimalist contents of his rucksack on the spare bed in his room. Staying in a dormitory would not give him such a luxury.

❖ ❖ ❖

By 4.30 pm both pilgrims had showered, sorted out their kit, and their combined laundry was in the receptionist's capable hands.

"Dunno about you John, but once I've done my personal admin thing I'm usually ready to have an hour's nap at this time of day," said Drew.

"Sounds like a great plan," said John, finally agreeing with something the old man said.

"I have a video call with Pete at six o'clock. Have you got anything for him?"

"Respect," said John, wryly.

Drew laughed, "Okay. I will give you a knock at seven, then we'll go out for dinner."

❖ ❖ ❖

Just before 6 pm Drew started a video meeting. After a few seconds the call connected showing Peter Dickinson with a golf course scene behind him.

"All right for some. Where are you, Dixie?" asked Drew.

"I'm in an awful sodding hotel in the middle of pigging Madrid, matey. This is just a photo of the Pebble Beach course which I use as my virtual backdrop, unless you really want to see my hotel room. Just had some ball-achingly tedious security meetings here today. Anyhow, how's it going?"

asked Peter.

Drew gave Peter a daily situation report on the journey and how John was coping. Or not coping.

"Do you think he'll make it?" asked Peter.

"To be honest, I didn't think he'd get here to Nájera, Dixie. He is Mister Grumpy."

"Oh well. Hopefully, it was just the after effects of the drinking session he had last night," said Peter. "He was so keen on doing the *Camino*, it was all he talked about for weeks. It was almost an obsession, but if he does quit we can get him into a clinic to detox. Just let me know.

"Meant to tell you that if you can't get hold of me for any reason, call my Global Security Operations Centre. It's in Pretoria but runs twenty-four hours a day. I will text you their phone number."

"Okay. Hope I don't ever need to use it, but thanks. Do the staff in the GSOC know about this operation?"

"No. They don't need to know, but just give them your codename and it should automatically trigger a planned response to get hold of me," said Peter.

"Makes sense. By the way, what is my codename?"

"Nursemaid," said Peter, giggling.

"Thanks a lot Dixie. I was rather hoping for something a bit more macho. On that note I will go and do an online recce of tomorrow's route, then wake up grouchy John and go for a meal."

"Okay Drew. Tomorrow I'll be out of comms during the day as I'm flying back to Joburg, but I should be ready for your sitrep at six."

"Oh alright. By the way, I withdrew two hundred *euros* from a cash machine today," said Drew.

"Thanks," said Peter, in a disinterested way, "do you have me confused with someone who gives a shit?"

"Just thought you should know, is all," said Drew, slightly taken aback.

"You don't need to tell me. You're in the Circle of Trust matey. I will check the travel card account every few days and top it up, so no worries. Anything from John for me?"

"Respect," said Drew, with a smile.

"Okay. Take care. Bye," said Peter, the video call ended.

Drew was puzzled. There was something missing from the meeting he just had with Peter and he could not quite figure out what it was.

After the video call, Drew collected the freshly laundered and folded clothes from reception; divided them up and left John's outside his door.

◆ ◆ ◆

At 7 pm Drew collected John and they took the short walk to Bar Franco II. It felt a lot further, now that their legs had stiffened up. When they entered the bar John instinctively took off his baseball cap.

"Keep it on please John," whispered Drew, as they shuffled to a table tucked away at the end of the counter.

Drew left John reading the menu card, while he went to the bar and bought *dos caña cerveza sin alcohol.*

Drew raised his glass to John, "Cheers!"

"*Gesondheid!*" said John. "I'm going to relish this beer. This is going to be my last one."

"Really?" said Drew. "Don't you like alcohol-free beer then?"

"Honestly? I wouldn't have known unless you told me, Andrew," said John, thinking that finding decent tasting alcohol-free beer was the highlight of a tediously tough day.

"And by the way, please call me Drew. Only my mother called me Andrew."

Drew ordered a few dishes of various *tapas* and a second round of what John called 'near beers.'

"So Drew, where are all the pilgrims?" asked John.

"We saw a few on The Way today from Logroño. I imagine most are having dinner in their *albergues* here in Nájera, either a communal meal or something they made. The mature couple we saw here as we came in are probably pilgrims as well."

"How can you tell?" asked John.

"They are dressed in pilgrim wear; the woman winced as she got up from the table and shambled painfully to the toilet; and the man has shorts and sandals with a well-developed suntan on his legs and brilliantly white feet with tape on his heels, so I'd say he has been wearing new ankle boots for a couple of weeks."

"You noticed all that?" said John, impressed with Drew's observational skills.

"Yes, all that. And the fact that when I was at the bar, I overheard them talking about tomorrow's route to Santo Domingo de la Calzada."

"So is this how we will continue on the *Camino*. Staying in hotels and dining out?" asked John, filling his plate with *patatas bravas, croquetas* and *pimientos de Padrón*.

"We could, but we kind of stand out. Our best way of going unnoticed may sound counter-intuitive: We need to immerse ourselves into the stream of pilgrims," said Drew. "So we're going to stay in *albergues* and blend into the crowd. They will be our camouflage. We will be like little fishes swimming along in the shoal."

"Okay. Oh, I meant to ask you. How did your video call go?" asked John.

"Funny thing about it that has been bugging me. If I was Peter, the one thing that I would be wanting to know at all times was our location. Where had we been? Where were we now? Pete never asked," said Drew.

"Why do you think he didn't ask?" said John.

"He doesn't need to ask..." said Drew, as he realised why, "because he already knows. He's tracking you, I reckon."

"Probably," said John, in an unemotional way.

"Everytime I'm back at home, Pete's IT guys give my phone, what they call a 'health check', but I've always suspected that they're probably updating some sort of tracking software."

"Okay. Good to know, but I don't think it's just on your phone. You switched it off, albeit somewhat reluctantly, this afternoon remember. So if that was the only method Peter could locate you, he would have gone crazy when you 'went dark.' He must have alternative ways to find out where you are. Has he given you any other technical devices?"

"Yeah, he gave me a special AirTag fob so if I ever lost my keys they could be located," said John, "and my ear buds can be located too. Should we be worried?"

"I think more reassured than worried," said Drew. "I guess I would have done the same. Multiple tracking devices, I'd call it a belt-and-braces approach."

"Onion skin," said John, finishing his food and draining his beer glass.

"What do you mean?"

"Pete is always banging on about the 'onion skin approach' to security. Layer upon layer of systems in place. The chance of one system failing is worryingly high, but multiple layers rarely fail," said John, repeating what Peter Dickinson had obviously told him.

Drew paid the bill and they left the bar.

♦ ♦ ♦

On their way back to the hostal John asked, "Why have I always got to keep this stupid cap on?"

"I'm concerned about facial recognition software. It might be CCTV or even someone innocently posting a photo of you on social media. If your identity gets compromised it might be a problem for us. So, if you can keep your hat on as much as you can that would be helpful. Have you considered growing a beard?" asked Drew.

"*Ag,* I don't get on with beards. They are okay for the first week, then the itching starts."

"Okay. Let's just go with the hat, and sunglasses too if possible."

When they returned to the hostal, John's painful climb up the stairs to the first floor was accompanied by sound effects.

"Oh, do put a sock in it John, you sound like an old man," said Drew, jokingly.

"You should know," said John. "You are an old man."

"I do hate cheeky kids," Drew responded in a friendly way. "Right, set your alarm for six thirty. We will leave at seven. Make sure your feet are dry before applying a bit of petroleum jelly. Helps prevent blisters."

"Okay, Good night, Drew."

4. NÁJERA TO SANTO DOMINGO

<u>577 km to Santiago de Compostela.</u>

Drew was awake before his 6.30 am alarm was due to go off. For a moment he lay in bed, thinking through the day. He tried to visualise the route, recounting the direction, distance, description, duration and destination of the day, while he smeared his toes and heels with petroleum jelly. The day had begun, no going back to sleep. He got up, got washed and dressed.

Out of habit, most of Drew's kit was already packed up, ready to go. He consulted his phone to reacquaint himself with the day's route and check for any messages. It was ominously quiet in the adjoining bedroom.

At 6.45 am Drew knocked on John's door. No reply.

"Morning John. You awake?" said Drew. No reply.

Drew banged on the door, "Wassup?" croaked John.

"Time to get up John. I leave in fifteen minutes," said Drew.

"What's the rush man?" said John, lazily. "I'm thinking more like eight am."

"And now, I leave in fourteen minutes," said Drew, emphatically.

◆ ◆ ◆

At 7 am Drew put on his rucksack and double-checked that he had not left anything behind in his bedroom or the bathroom. Still no sounds of activity from the next bedroom.

Drew knocked on the door, said, "Goodbye John," and left the hotel.

At Bar Franco II, Drew ordered a *café cortado* and a slice of *tortilla de patatas*, served with a piece of crusty bread. He sat at a table and watched people walk by in the early morning sunshine. The coffee tasted rich. The gooey *tortilla* was still warm. Life was good.

Out of habit Drew tucked the bread into his food bag for later. He had finished the *tortilla* and was about to swig the last of his coffee when he saw a figure hurrying past the bar.

"*Buenos dias peregrino*," Drew said from the front door.

John stopped and turned around, an expression of relief and annoyance on his face, "Very funny, Andrew."

"Good morning sleepy. Take a seat. I'll get you a coffee, orange juice and some *tortilla*," said Drew.

"What's *tortilla*?" said John, petulantly.

"If you like potatoes, onions, garlic and eggs - you'll love *tortilla*. And put your bloody cap on," said Drew as he went to the counter. John was annoying Drew. A lot.

After a few minutes Drew returned and served John his breakfast.

"Why did you bloody leave me? My father would be so furious if he heard that my bodyguard had deserted me. Absolutely furious," said John, seething.

"What's your daddy going to do? Fire me?" laughed Drew. "Listen, you've been used to having everything done for you, all your life. So I can't blame you for thinking that I'm at your beck and call, but if I say get up at six thirty and we leave at seven that's what we'll do. And, by the way, I'm still not your bodyguard," Drew controlled the urge to add an excessive amount of profanity and violent sexual imagery into his language to reinforce his message.

"So you're not going to take a bullet for me?" asked John, mockingly.

"If that's what you want, you need a close protection team. I think we should establish the ground rules so I can manage your expectations. I'm here as a pilgrim on my way to Santiago," said Drew as John sipped his *café con leche.* "I will look out for threats and try to warn you if I can, but you must also be on the lookout. It is a partnership.

"If you get into trouble I will try and help you, if I can. If I get attacked, I want you to get to somewhere safe. I mean a place where the paying public are being served, like a café, restaurant, shop, petrol station or bar.

"So. Have you got everything from your hotel room?" asked Drew, changing the subject.

"Yes," said John, sulking.

"And was the *tortilla* to your liking?"

"It was okay," said John, "I suppose."

"Wonderful. Simply wonderful," said Drew. He packed his rucksack and, when John was finished, he took all of the crockery back to the counter.

"Let's walk," said Drew.

❖ ❖ ❖

They set off, across the bridge over the river and followed the yellow arrows through the historic old town.

It was a steep walk out of Nájera and the pair took it steady. The weather was similar to the previous day. Drew would be removing his windcheater soon as he warmed up.

They heard a British couple chatting to each other as they approached them from behind. With only a small day pack each, the pair easily outpaced Drew and John.

John said, "I presume they are having their heavy stuff transported ahead."

"Oh yes. And staying in comfortable hotels; all *ensuite* bathrooms, with soft beds, a choice of pillows and fluffy towels I expect," said Drew, with just a hint of envy.

❖ ❖ ❖

After walking for a couple of kilometres in silence, Drew said, "I have a present for you."

"Is it a time machine?" said John, hopefully.

"Nope. Better than that."

"Woo-hoo, what could be better than a time machine? A magic lantern? With a genie who can grant me three wishes?" said John, with as much sarcasm as he could inject.

"Good guess... but wrong. It's a *credential*."

"A what?"

"A pilgrim passport, ta-da!" said Drew, handing John the cardboard folded leaflet with a flourish. "Get a stamp a day, two a day during your last hundred kilometres, and you present it at Santiago and you get your soul cleansed from mortal sin. A spotless soul - what a gift!"

"Er, yeah. I suppose," said John, somewhat underwhelmed.

"Just keep it in the plastic bag with your passport. You'll need it to get into *albergues*."

❖ ❖ ❖

They had reached the top of the climb out of Nájera.

"What have you been told about me?" asked John, to break the monotony of the walking.

"Peter said that you had been having a rough

time coping with life after the, er... kidnap."

"You can say that again," said John.

Drew resisted the urge to repeat what he had just said verbatim. "And that you wanted to walk The Way of Saint James instead of detoxing in a rehabilitation clinic."

"Did he tell you how much I'm worth?" asked John.

"Nope. And, quite frankly, I'm not bothered. You can have enough money to buy 'The moon on a stick' if you want, but who cares?" said Drew.

The pair continued walking in relative silence. The heat of the day built up.

"Time for a break I think," said Drew, after an hour or so. He put his rucksack down, got out a couple of apples and granola bars and handed one of each to John.

Drew took off his boots and socks. He stretched his legs out in the morning sunshine.

After yesterday's foot care lecture, John reluctantly followed Drew's example.

"Sun feels good on my feet. Should dry them out nicely," said John.

Drew processed what he had just heard, "Did you shower this morning?"

"Of course," said John, slightly indignant.

"My mistake. I mustn't have explained this. On *Camino* we don't shower in the morning, it causes the skin on the feet to be soft and susceptible to blisters. Here, have this microfibre towel and dry them off thoroughly, and change your socks."

After John had begrudgingly dried his feet, he rubbed them with a bit of petroleum jelly and put on fresh dry socks.

"Your feet look blister free. Let's walk," said Drew.

❖ ❖ ❖

Some time later.

"It's not fair," said John, testily.

"Okay," Drew replied, apathetically, "what's not fair?"

"You've got a walking stick and I haven't," John sounded more like a spoiled brat than an adult.

Drew stopped, slipped off his rucksack and got out a spare trekking pole. He clicked the three tubular sections together and adjusted the clamp so that the length was suitable for John.

"May I award you with your very own trekking pole. It won't rust, bust, pick up dust, buckle or bend," said Drew, handing it to John horizontally as if he was presenting him with the sword of honour. He adjusted the wrist strap and showed him how to put his hand through it the correct way.

"Can my father not afford two?" asked John.

Bloody ingrate! thought Drew. "If you want another one we can get you one. I just think that the experts at countryside walking are farmers and shepherds. They only ever use one stick."

The pair continued through the countryside

and small villages.

♦ ♦ ♦

The Seat Ibiza missed the entrance to the hotel's underground car park in Palencia, about 200 kilometres from Drew and John, for the second time.

"Juan, you're a total embarrassment," said the passenger with a *madrilleños* accent.

"I blame your useless directions Isabella. How about we just call this an 'anti-surveillance drill' eh?" said Juan discourteously, as he drove the car up to the intercom, finally. He explained that they had reservations and the shutters were opened remotely.

As the couple removed their luggage, Juan complained, "Why didn't we get a SUV 4×4, rather than this toy car?"

"This car is more discreet. It will blend in nicely. Stop complaining, remember who's in charge here," said Isabella, coldly.

At reception Juan and Isabella were booked into their respective rooms, with an interconnecting door.

Juan settled into his bedroom, logged onto the WiFi, checked his personal social media accounts, before heading off to the gym.

♦ ♦ ♦

At Cirueña, Drew and John stopped at a bar,

after about four hours of steady walking. They had coffee and refilled their water bottles.

"You know you make a rehab clinic an enticing prospect?" John said, glumly.

"What's the matter?"

"I'm not sure this is for me, Drew. Sorry to have wasted your time, but I think I will quit."

"Don't worry about me, John. I would have been here, walking the *Camino*, anyway."

"So, you're not going to try and talk me out of bailing out?" asked John, slightly surprised.

"Nope. You're an adult, not a child. Your decision. If you want to take your aura on a journey of self-discovery and bugger off somewhere else; sit on a beach; climb Killamanjaro; work on a *kibbutz;* whatever - knock yourself out," said Drew.

"Oh," said John, who had expected Drew to talk him out of giving up. "Do you ever feel like throwing in the towel?" asked John, drinking his coffee.

"Most days, yes," Drew laughed. "I usually say to myself 'Tomorrow. I will give up tomorrow.'"

"What's the point in it? Just monotonous walking. Day after day," said John.

"Not enough stimulation for a Gen Zed type like you?" said Drew, finishing his coffee. "It is tough, both physically and mentally. I find that when I've finished a *Camino* I get a feeling that I have succeeded in something special. 'Mission accomplished' you could say."

"I imagined the *Camino* would be so much better than it really is. So far it's just been *kak*!"

"Maybe it helps if you are more of a realist than, er..." said Drew, trying to find the right word.

"An optimist?" John offered.

"Yes. An optimist. I'm your typical glass half empty sort of bloke. I expect travel cockups, crap weather, bad food, cold showers, no bed - so if anything good, pleasant or nice happens, I think of it as a blessing."

"You are a true pilgrim. This really is a bloody penance for ya."

"Well I suppose if you treat the *Camino* like a penance, you may enjoy it more. The question of what constitutes a 'true pilgrim' - phew! How long have you got?" laughed Drew, as he finished packing his rucksack and strapping it on.

Just then a young woman with a NY Yankees baseball cap sat down with a bright and breezy, "*Hola!*"

"Oh hello. Sorry to be rude, but we're just leaving. *Buen Camino*," said Drew, to the *peregrina*. "Let's walk," he said to John.

"Seriously? Was it something I said?" bleated the woman, as the two pilgrims walked away.

"Really? Seriously!" she shouted after them with exasperation.

A couple of kilometres outside of Cirueña, Drew asked John, "So, are you still going to quit?"

"Definitely. You're damned right I'm going to quit," said John. "Tomorrow."

◆ ◆ ◆

It was a very sad day in the Cleveland Clinic Cancer Center, Ohio. After a year of valiant struggle against bowel cancer Pat Kavanagh, the immensely popular patient in room 9, passed away peacefully.

Pat's son, Noel, removed his father's effects and returned them to his home. He faced the daunting prospect of disposing of the contents of the apartment, including hundreds of reels of old film and video tapes from a lifetime of working as a cameraman.

5. SANTO DOMINGO DE LA CALZADA

On the way into Santo Domingo de la Calzada, Drew and John bought a bag full of groceries from the *Dia supermercado*. They made their way along Calle Mayor and stopped at the first *albergue.*

"Have you got reservations?" said John.

Drew resisted the temptation to say that he had plenty of reservations about staying at an *albergue* with John, but instead said, "Nope. We will just see if it's true that the *Camino* provides." As they lined up behind a couple of pilgrims who were already checking in with the *hospitalera*.

Drew did not want to tempt fate by slipping off his rucksack or removing his boots. If the *albergue* was full they would have to keep going.

"*Buenas tardes, dos camas por favor*?" asked Drew.

"*Si*," said the *hospitalera* accepting the passports and *credentials* from Drew and John. She stamped Drew's *credential*, which was filled with stamps starting from Saint-Jean-Pied-de-Port in France. The *hospitalera* looked at John's brand-new *credential* and put the first stamp in it saying, "*Tu primero.*"

Drew paid cash and took directions from the *hospitalera*. The pilgrims put their trekking poles in the bucket in the drying room. Took off their boots and, after stuffing them with old newspaper, placed them on the rack. They put on their sandals and went up to the dormitory.

"Top or bottom?" asked Drew, pointing at their bunk bed.

"Top," said John, about to swing his rucksack onto the top mattress, before he heard Drew making a throat clearing sound. Ah, yes he remembered about bed bugs. He put his rucksack on the floor and followed Drew's example.

Drew put the awkward paper sheet on his mattress, the paper cover on his pillow and stretched out his quilt from his pack on his bed. Once done, he found his wash kit and clean clothes, before heading for the showers.

After they were showered, John was given a coaching session in washing his clothes in a deep sink, rinsing them a couple of times to get the soap out, wringing them semi-dry before pegging them out on the washing line.

They shared the room with a couple of retired Danish nurses, a young Spaniard from Tarragona and a 70-year-old German Catholic priest, with sleep apnoea.

Drew learnt that the priest was one of five brothers and it was their father's dearest wish to join the priesthood. However, according to his father, his mother was too beautiful. The priest admitted that he did not walk far each day. About ten to fifteen kilometres, but he walked in sandals and carried his burden of a CPAP machine to help him breathe at night.

◆ ◆ ◆

To act like other pilgrims, Drew and John sauntered along to the Cathedral which had an illuminated coop with two white chickens.

"What's with these chickens?" said John, pointing to the coop.

"It's a famous story about a local young woman a long time ago who fancied the son of a German couple who were on pilgrimage. The young lad spurned her advances and she planted a silver cup on him to get him into trouble."

"I'm guessing it didn't end well for the boy."

"And you'd be right. He was tried, convicted, executed and left hanging here while the parents went on their merry way to Santiago, as you would," said Drew, incredulously.

"And the chickens?" asked John, as the Danish nurses they were to share their dormitory with walked past.

"I'm just getting to that part. Mum and Dad, on their way back from seeing Saint James, paid their respects to the body of their son and found that he was still very much alive. They rushed to the Mayor, who was having a dinner of roast chickens, to tell him the good news. To which he reacted by saying 'The lad is no more alive than these plump breasted chickens I'm about to scoff.' Or words to that effect. At which point, believe it or not, the chickens got up and flew away."

"So what happened next?" asked John.

"I imagine the Mayor had to have baked beans on toast."

"No, *Moegoe*. What happened to the chickens?"

"Oh yes. Since that time the locals have kept chickens in the cathedral. Apparently, it is a blessing if a feather lands on you," said Drew.

"And if one craps on top of your head?" asked John.

"Good luck."

"Why is that good luck?" asked John.

"Good luck that you weren't looking up at the time," Drew said, laughing quietly.

As they walked around the cathedral, Drew took careful note of pilgrims and tourists in case they were being followed.

◆ ◆ ◆

Juan returned to his Palencia hotel room from the gym. Took a shower. Put on a fresh T-shirt and shorts. Checked his phone for messages. Watched the sports channels on the flat screen TV, with a small beer from the minibar.

At 4 pm exactly he knocked twice on the interconnecting door. Isabella opened the door while she was talking on her phone. She waved

Juan in and indicated that he should sit in the chair by the desk.

"Yes Chief, we are at the hotel. The tech is working well... Yes the tracker is pinging..." said Isabella.

Juan saw that the laptop, on the desk, had photos of John De Witt and Andrew Mallam on the screen. On the bedroom TV was a map of Northern Spain with a flashing icon at Santo Domingo de la Calzada. Also on the desk was a bag with radios and what looked like gloves and handcuffs.

When Isabella finished the call she said to Juan, "Memorise the faces of the targets," in a peevish tone. Something, or someone, was causing her irritation. Juan was soon to find out it was him.

"I do like a woman to be in control. What else is in your bag of kinky kit?" Juan's cheekiness had just crossed the line.

"Let's get this straight, Juan," said Isabella in a no-nonsense tone. "You're here for driving and muscle when things get 'tactical' in the final phase. While you're on this job - no drinking, I can smell it on you.

"And when you come into this room you will be dressed ready to deploy, not in your gym kit. One word from me to the Chief and you'll be back in the *Costa* nightclub or whichever shithole you came from. *Claro*?"

"*Claro*. Loud and clear," said Juan, in a subdued voice.

"Also in the bag are covert earpieces, pepper

spray, handcuffs and," Isabella said pulling a black cylindrical object out, "this is an extendable baton, just in case you got it confused with anything else. Just keep your mind on the mission."

◆ ◆ ◆

Drew found a shaded corner of the garden at the *albergue* and fitted wired earpieces to his phone. Just after 6 pm Drew started a video meeting. Peter answered in front of the same golf course background.

"See you're still on the golf course Dixie," said Drew.

"Yes, I'll be there in a year or so when I've finally pulled the pin and retired from this game. Anyway, how's today gone?"

Drew gave Peter a run down on the day so far. Peter complained about the travel from Madrid back to Johannesburg.

"So any scandal, gossip, rumour or smut?" asked Peter.

"Nope. Just got a nagging doubt that this is all going to go belly-up, Dixie."

"How do you mean?" asked Peter.

"Well I'm just not convinced that John's heart is in it. Today was a slow start for him. Think he will just throw the towel in and quit."

"You've gotta remember that the lad's never been in the military, never enjoyed the 'structure' we've had through our basic training," said Peter, knowing that most of the time he derived no enjoyment at all from being ordered around night and day.

"Do you mean the discipline of a regiment?"

"Yes. He's had everything given to him on a plate, all of his life. It's not his fault, but he's been spoiled. He might need a bit of..."

"Positive encouragement?" Drew offered.

"Exactly, and good luck with that. I'm off to do a bit of light emailing, then get an early night," then Peter said with a smile, "Give John my love. See ya Nursemaid."

"Get stuffed," said Drew lightheartedly, terminating the meeting.

Drew concluded that John was definitely being tracked by Dixie as, again, no questions were asked about his location.

Whether or not John continued on the *Camino* was in the balance. Peter did not seem concerned either way. Drew felt that if John did give up he would not want to be to blame so dedicated to continue being a supportive mentor. Maybe a home-cooked supper would help cement the bond between them, he thought.

❖ ❖ ❖

"I'll prepare us dinner tonight," said Drew to John back in the dormitory. "Join me in the kitchen when you feel like it."

"You're a chef as well? There's no end to your

talents Drew."

To manage John's expectations, Drew said, "After you've tasted my food you might change your mind and say that there is no 'beginning' to my talents."

In the kitchen of the *albergue* another couple of pilgrims, Enzo and Antonia from Italy, were busying themselves with food preparation as well. Antonia wore a bright blue top with a yellow arrow and the words *Camino de Santiago*.

Drew boiled four eggs, while he put out a ready-made green salad and threw on some chunks of feta cheese and a few anchovies.

John joined him in the kitchen and tucked into the salad as Drew boiled some spaghetti, fried bacon pancetta, drained the pasta and added it to the bacon, took it off the heat, added two egg yolks and mixed it well.

"Hey presto, *Spaghetti a la Carbonara*," said Drew as he dished it out onto two plates.

"Well done chef. Would have been better with a bit of *Parmesan* cheese," said John, ruefully.

Enzo overhead John and offered him and Drew some grated *Parmigiano Reggiano* to sprinkle on top.

"*Grazie mille*," said Drew to the Italian.

"*Tu capisci l'italiano*?" asked Enzo.

"*Mi dispiace*. I just know a few words. That's all. Where are you from?" asked Drew.

"Genova. You call it Genoa. Have you been there?" asked Enzo.

"Yes. The Genoans have a certain reputation for being..." Drew was not sure how to end the sentence without causing offence.

"...careful with our money?" suggested Antonia, laughing.

"Yes. Thank you. I was going to say 'skilled in business matters,'" said Drew.

The Italians made light of the fact that the good people of Genoa are famous for their financial prudence.

"Cheers," said Drew to John, as he toasted his good health with a glass of water.

John replied, "*Gesondheid!*"

"Ah! You are German," said Antonia.

"No, South African actually," said John. He could sense Drew's displeasure.

After they had finished their meal Drew took the plates and cutlery to the sink, leaving John talking with the Italian couple. As he returned to the table Enzo had just taken a selfie with him, Antonia and John.

"I fancy stretching my legs with a stroll. Are you up for that Drew?" asked John.

"Yes. I will just check to see if our clothes are dry first."

◆ ◆ ◆

Drew and John walked out of the *albergue* and around the town. The evening was still pleasantly warm and they took in the old architecture.

Eventually they sat at a table in a quiet bar on the *Plaza España*.

"Is there any moral to the story about the chickens in the cathedral?" asked John.

"I dunno. Beware of manipulative predatory young women maybe," offered Drew.

"Hell hath no fury like a woman scorned, eh?" said John.

"No comment," said Drew. "A toast to all women. God bless them, every one."

"Yes. God bless them. Cheers!" said John. "I will avoid saying *gesondheid*. When I said it in the *albergue* I could feel you staring at me. But you'll never get me to say 'God save the King!'"

"So, first impressions of *albergue* living?" Drew asked.

"Fairly straightforward," said John.

Drew went through the dos and don'ts of the nighttime routine in a shared dormitory and the anticipation of snorers.

"So if we get a few hours of decent sleep, consider it a blessing," said Drew.

John was then briefed to creep out of the dormitory and get into the kitchen to pack up in the morning, so as not to disturb anyone.

"Got any worries?" asked Drew.

"Nope. Have you?" asked John.

"Just got a concern about you being photographed by the Italians."

"They seemed friendly. Shared their food. Even offered us their wine. Are you paranoid?"

asked John.

"I've got no issue with them. My worry is what will Enzo do with the photo he took?"

"He can't tag it on his social media posts with my name because I didn't give him it. Don't worry man."

"Yeah. I'm overthinking things, as usual. Anyway I'm ready for an early night," said Drew, finishing his drink. "Let's walk."

◆ ◆ ◆

Like many millions of others that day, a digital image was processed. The location details of the phone which took the picture, as well as the time and date, were attached automatically to the metadata for that photograph.

The program recognised three faces and, in milliseconds, measured the distances between features such as eyes, nose and mouth, before converting each face into a string of zeros and ones to create digital 'fingerprints.'

Other software programs were continuously scanning social media sites to sniff out certain faces - personalities, celebrities, politicians, even wayward spouses. A match was found.

Several accounts around the world were interested in any image which showed the face of John de Witt, heir to the De Witt fortune. Alerts landed in a number of email accounts, reporting that at 19.34 hours John de Witt was at Calle

Mayor, Santo Domingo de la Calzada, La Rioja, Spain.

The photograph clearly showed a happy group of three casually dressed people having dinner. The woman was wearing a T-shirt with an arrow logo and *Camino de Santiago* emblazoned on the front. Many of the alerts were simply ignored and deleted. Some were not.

6. SANTO DOMINGO TO CASTILDELGARDO

<u>556 km to Santiago de Compostela.</u>

Drew and John left the *albergue* at 6.30 am. At first they thought that the main street had been washed overnight, but the sad realisation was that it had been raining. And there was more rain to come.

The city streets led to a country track and Drew had to use his head torch.

"Can't you see where you're going *Ouballie*?" asked John, breaking the silence.

"I just don't want to trip or sprain an ankle," and added as an afterthought, "or step in any dog crap."

"You didn't think to bring a head torch for me?" asked John, crossly.

"We should be okay just with the light from mine."

About a kilometre from Santo Domingo de la Calzada, Drew could see the torch light from a cluster of pilgrims ahead. He turned around to look back to the town and was amused at the sight of at least a dozen head torches in a line of pilgrims bobbing up and down in the dark.

Drew hoped that the rain would hold off. It did not.

The pair stopped as the drizzle turned into proper rain. They put covers on their rucksacks and their waterproof jackets on. Welcome to the *Camino Frances*, thought Drew.

◆ ◆ ◆

Dawn eventually broke and the rain abated. Drew and John could pack away their waterproofs, but left the covers on their packs.

As they headed towards Grañón, John pointed out to Drew that the pilgrims ahead were walking on the wrong side of the road.

"Yes. I agree with you John. We should walk on the left so we can face oncoming traffic," said Drew, "but you've got to remember we need to fit in with everyone else. We are the little fishes in the shoal."

They continued to plod on, on the right.

As the pilgrims crossed the main road in Redecilla del Camino they dropped into the tourist office. Inside the receptionist made them coffee and they sat at a large table with only one other customer, the young woman with a NY Yankees baseball cap they had met briefly the day before.

"Ya don't speak much, do ya?" said the American to John.

"Well he's not the talkative sort and definitely he's not as interesting as me," butted in Drew. "You from the East Coast?"

"You're damn right, but hey, let me decide if the young dude ain't interesting. He looks interesting to me," she persisted.

"Ah, but looks can be deceptive," parried Drew, trying to finish his hot coffee quickly. "Come on partner, let's get going. We need a pharmacy to get that medication."

"Oh yeah. What's wrong with you?" said the young woman.

"Not me madam, but junior here has awful haemorrhoids," Drew cringed dramatically, "simply awful. Ugh."

Undeterred the young woman said, "Well at least tell me your name before ya go. I'm Ellen."

The two men slid their rucksacks on and adjusted their straps, "John. My name is John."

Ellen smiled, "See ya later... John."

◆ ◆ ◆

Later, Drew explained to John why he had stonewalled the interest from Ellen. "There are millions of reasons why pilgrims walk the *Camino*, but a common one is that they are in-between relationships. She may be vulnerable and you wouldn't want to take advantage of her situation would you?"

"We'd call her a *loskind*, back home," said John.

"Whatever that means," said Drew. "Anyway you don't want to get involved, she may only have a rucksack, but you don't know how much other 'baggage' she's packing, if you know what I mean. Any which way, she's going to be a distraction from you getting clean."

"You just don't want me to have any fun. And now Ellen thinks I have haemorrhoids."

"Wonder who put that idea into her pretty little head," said Drew, with a not so innocent grin.

❖ ❖ ❖

As they were about to leave the village of Castildelgardo, Drew noticed an open door to the chapel and a sign welcoming pilgrims. To keep the pilgrim appearance going, Drew and John entered the simply decorated chapel and were welcomed by an elderly bearded priest wearing a padded jacket and sandals. He smiled, offered Drew a small lit candle and indicated for him to put it at the altar.

Drew tried to get some money out as a donation, but the little priest shook his head.

John just stood back and watched Drew place the candle and stand in reverential silence for a couple of minutes.

As he returned to the door the priest showed him a piece of paper which had written in English an offer for him to receive a blessing. Again, he tried to make a donation. Again, the priest refused.

Drew bowed his head and the priest laid one hand on his forehead and said a long blessing aloud in Spanish, or it could have been Latin.

Eventually the blessing was finished. Drew smiled and the little old priest hugged him.

With a, "*Muchas gracias Padre*," Drew left the chapel with John.

After a while, John said, "Feel better?"

"To be honest I felt that the blessing was really special. I was so moved I nearly lost it back there John."

"What? You nearly cried?" asked John.

"Yep. Dunno what was going on, but the cheese nearly fell off my cracker."

7. CASTILDELGARDO TO BELORADO

The pilgrims passed through Viloria del Rioja and walked on the quiet country road which joins the main N-120, connecting Burgos to Logroño.

Drew and John overtook a mature Spanish couple who were strolling along. They smiled and all wished each other, "*Buen Camino.*"

Shortly afterwards, as Drew and John trudged along the road, Drew said, "Did you see that?"

"No. What?" said John, hoping for anything to break the monotony of the morning. He was about to get far more than he bargained for.

"A car up ahead has just driven off and there are two dogs barking their heads off at it. Can't figure out if the car had stopped to avoid hitting the dogs, or the car driver had just thrown the dogs out. I didn't see what happened."

At the T-junction 150 metres ahead, two lively dogs were chasing each other around playfully. There was no alternative route. The pilgrims would have to pass the dogs, a small yappy mongrel terrier type and a more docile leggy black dog which Drew could not quite recognise yet.

Neither pilgrim was afraid of dogs. Drew

and John discussed the best way to pass them. They decided to walk confidently, looking straight ahead, so as not to make threatening eye contact. Some dogs have been treated badly and hate people carrying sticks. Others do not like uniforms. So the pilgrims removed their hats and hid their trekking poles vertically by their sides to make themselves look less intimidating.

They were a few metres from the junction when the dogs became aware of the pilgrims. The dogs were still playing, the smaller one running rings around the black one.

"I think the big one is a Doberman," said Drew.

"Uh ho. We had one of those as a guard dog at one of our facilities and it attacked an intruder," said John, cautiously.

"I assume it taught the intruder a valuable lesson he would never forget," said Drew, trying to lighten the mood.

"It was his last lesson in fact. Those dogs are bred to 'strike low,'" said John.

"You mean attack the groin?"

"Yep. We say the *balla*," said John. An *Afrikaaner* word that Drew did not need to have translated.

Both Drew and John instinctively put their hands in front of them, to protect their 'family jewels.' Walking side-by-side they looked like footballers forming a pathetic freekick wall.

The mongrel terrier, or a '*brak*' as John called it, made the first sortie, yapping its way past them quickly and circling around to sniff them.

"*Perro tranquilo*," said Drew to the mongrel, hoping it was impressed by his mastery of the Spanish language.

The Doberman was a more wary beast. It slunk along and, as it passed, its lip curled to expose its ugly teeth. Drew assessed the risks. The mongrel could give them a nasty nip, but the Doberman was akin to a 'land-shark' and gave him a chill.

"Phew! I'm glad they're gone," said John, as the two dogs carried on down the road behind them, yapping away.

"I didn't like that Doberman one little bit. Bloody evil looking thing," said Drew.

As they put their hats back on and got into their stride, they heard the barking intensify and a Spanish man shout, "*Vamos! Vamos!*"

Drew turned and saw the Spanish pilgrim couple were being circled by the dogs. The man was kicking out frantically at the small mongrel and using his trekking poles like sabres, to slash the air.

Drew turned to face forward and a couple of seconds later heard a woman screaming. He turned once more and saw both dogs were running away, deafened by the high-pitched screech. The woman had her hands clasped around her face, like Edvard Munch's most famous painting. She had dropped her trekking poles in the road. The man was perfectly still. Drew could not fathom what had occurred. There was something odd about the man's trousers. Drew focused in on the detail. One trouser leg was beige, the other Burgundy red. The penny dropped, Drew figured out what had just happened and ran towards the couple.

The Spaniard was clutching his groin, as Drew got to him. Blood pulsing over the man's hands.

"Lie down. Lie down," said Drew, as he helped the man to sit down on the road, then lie back against his rucksack.

The woman had stopped screaming and was now shouting a stream of incomprehensible Spanish, including the word, "*Alfonso,*" which Drew took to be her husband's name.

Drew had to slow the catastrophic bleed, and fast.

"*Alfonso. Vale. Vale,*" said Drew, in as calming a way as he could. Straddling Alfonso's left leg he undid the belt and started to tug his trousers down. Alfonso had a vice-like grip on his trousers, but it would not prevent him bleeding to death in minutes. Drew's hands were now slippery with warm bright red arterial blood and getting wetter by the second.

"*Ag* man! What can I do?" said John, as he jogged in to join them.

"Grab the guy's arms and pull his hands away. I gotta try and stop the bleed."

John ripped Alfonso's hands away from his groin, Drew dragged his trousers to his ankles. It was a bloody mess. The Doberman's teeth had punctured the man's femoral artery.

Alfonso shouted expletives in Spanish and his wife shrieked as she saw blood pulsing out of the wound in the cleft of her husband's groin. Drew could see where he needed to apply pressure and knew what he would need to do. If it was going to work, it was going to be brutal.

"*Lo siento*," said Drew as he pushed down hard on the wound with his left hand, applying more and more pressure until the bleeding stopped. Alfonso shouted in pain.

"John, get his rucksack off him and lie him down flat. Hold him down if you have to," there was no time to think. Alfonso was groaning and the woman had now turned on Drew, shouting at him to get off her husband.

John had taken Alfonso's rucksack off and laid him down as he was groaning, "*Oh dios! Oh dios!*" John saw the woman berating Drew, so he pulled her towards her husband and said, "Alfonso. Alfonso." This was like the magic word and she knelt by her husband's head talking to him, like a mother cooing to her baby.

"*Buena! Buena!*" said Drew to the woman. Then he raised his right hand to his head as if he was holding a phone and said, "*Ambulancia?*"

"What can I do?" said John.

"Can you see where my left hand is?" asked Drew, pointing at the grisly scene.

"Yes. I think so," said John, hoping Drew was not going to ask him to get any closer.

"Don't worry. It'll be fine, as long as I keep the

pressure on the artery. I'm only going to release when we have medics here who can stem the bleed professionally, or..."

"Or what?" said John.

"Or... if I pass out," Drew said. "If I faint, stick the heel of your hand here, right into the groin, where the dog bite is."

"Okay, but don't faint, man. What can I do now?" asked John.

"You must keep your hands clear of the blood," Drew instructed.

"To prevent infection?" asked John.

"No, to work your damn phone. Get the translation app and find out what 'femoral artery bleed' is in Spanish, then keep it handy. And while you're doing nothing else," said Drew, facetiously, "keep a lookout for traffic. I don't want us all to get creamed along the tarmac by a truck from the main road."

The woman had connected with the emergency ambulance service and was sobbing her way through the details with the operator.

Drew said, *"Buena Señora. Ambulancia rapida. Muy importante, rapida."* He smiled at her and put his thumb up to encourage her. The sight of Drew's blood covered hand just upset her even more. Alfonso was still groaning and now pleading, *"Agua favor. Agua."*

John had the translation on his phone, *arteria femoral sangrar.* "Good man. Show it to the woman," said Drew. John waggled his phone in front of the woman who repeated the words to the ambulance operator.

"Keep that on your phone John," said Drew, thinking he might need the phrase again. "What time is it?"

"It's ten thirty-four," said John.

With the tip of his right finger Drew wrote 10.34 on Alfonso's white T-shirt in blood.

The woman took the man's water bottle from his rucksack and flipped open the lid. "*Sin agua,*" Drew said to the woman, shaking his head, "*Sin agua.*"

Further down the road, Drew saw a group of three pilgrims heading their way. "John. Speak to those pilgrims. If any of them is a doctor, or first aid trained, invite them to join the party," said Drew.

"And if not?" asked John.

"Get them onto the far side of the road and tell them not to look. I can do without more problems on my hands."

The bleeding had mostly stopped. Drew found it difficult keeping his hand on the right spot in the slippery, bloody cleft of Alfonso's groin. Enough pressure to stem the bleed, but not so much to cut off the flow of blood along the artery entirely. He kept smiling at the couple and making reassuring noises, "*Vale. Ambulancia rapida. Bueno.*"

John escorted the three pilgrims onto the far side of the road. "Did you warn them about those dogs?" said Drew, when he returned.

"No, dammit. Should I have done?"

"No," said Drew with a smile. "The dogs are probably still running, with their ears ringing. I think the artery is just punctured, rather than severed."

"Yeah, that is good news. How do you know?" said John.

"If it was severed we would have lost him by now."

A van pulled up from the main road and the driver got out. He stubbed out his cigarette and walked over to offer his assistance.

"John, show the guy the translation will you," directed Drew.

The van driver could now see Alfonso and what appeared to be a bucket's worth of blood splashed on the road. He saw Drew, soaked in blood, kneeling by the casualty. John showed the van driver the translation, *arteria femoral sangrar*. The man looked shocked, he spoke to Drew in Spanish. Drew shook his head. Alfonso's wife spoke to the driver and Drew heard the word, "*Ambulancia.*" The man gave a weak smile and put his hands together, as if in prayer. He got back into his van, put the hazard lights on and parked it at an angle on the road.

"How are you doing man?" said John to Drew.

"I've had better days," said Drew. The scene was protected from traffic by the van, Alfonso was still conscious, the blood loss was stemmed, an ambulance was on its way and the woman had stopped screaming. Drew did not know how long he could keep the pressure on the artery before the leg was lost, "What time is it now?"

"Ten forty-one," said John.

"Okay. So it's been seven minutes since I applied the pressure. Do you have any first aid knowledge?"

"*Ja*. What needs doing?" asked John.

"Nothing... at the moment. The fact is I can't move until we have help on site to stop the bleed. So poor old Alfonso has got to remain on his back. He must stay awake or-" said Drew.

"He will swallow his tongue?" interrupted John.

"In a way, yes. If he loses consciousness you are going to have to keep his airway open. Do you know how to do that?" asked Drew.

"I could do a head tilt," said John.

"Yeah, that should do the trick. Whatever happens, we are not losing him. Got it?" said Drew, confidently.

"Got it. I'll try and make sure he stays awake," said John.

The minutes passed like hours. Several cars slowed down to gawp, but the van driver encouraged them to move on, with colourful colloquial Spanish.

"John, go to the main road and if you see an ambulance, wave like hell," said Drew.

Eventually, Drew heard a siren. It got louder and louder. He had never been so happy to see an ambulance in his life.

One paramedic rushed to the scene with a suitcase size medic kit. She assessed the situation. John showed her the translation on his phone. She nodded, saw exactly where Drew's left hand was and said quietly to him, "*Quédate ahí.*"

"*No hablo español. Lo siento. Ingles,*" said Drew, apologetically.

The paramedic thought carefully, then said in a whisper, "No fucking move."

"*Vale,*" said Drew, nodding vigorously.

She introduced herself to Alfonso, "*Hola, soy Sina,*" and reassured him that he would be alright. Alfonso spoke weakly to Sina and Drew thought he heard him say, "*Perro diablo bastardo malvado.*"

A male paramedic with Pedro on his name badge, joined Sina and they donned aprons, clear plastic face masks and long disposable gloves. Pedro set up an intravenous drip into Alfonso's arm to replace the volume of fluid he had lost. His wife held the bag of saline solution.

Sina said to Drew, "How long?" and pointed to her watch and Drew's hand on the wound.

Drew pointed to the man's T-shirt with 10.34 in blood. Sina nodded and set herself up around Drew, again making it very clear that he must stay perfectly still. She laid out various dressings to get to them quickly.

Pedro spoke softly to Alfonso and his wife. The paramedics brought professional calmness to the crisis. Alfonso received an injection from Pedro, which seemed to calm him down. Ketamine, thought Drew.

The van driver and John did their bit to keep onlookers away from the scene and help bring the stretcher from the ambulance.

The paramedics looked at each other. It was time. Sina wagged her finger at Drew, "No move yet. *Muy importante.*"

"*Si,*" said Drew, nodding.

"When I say. You go. *Claro?*" said the paramedic. Drew again nodded in agreement.

Pedro indicated for John to get Alfonso's wife to look away. She would not want to see what came next. Sina chose a blood-clotting dressing, put it back down, chose a bigger one and unwrapped it. Breathing slowly she said to herself, "*Dios ayúdame.*" With the dressing she made a sign of the cross and looked into Drew's eyes.

"*Vamos!*" she said sharply to Drew and shouldered him away. Having been in one position for so long Drew had seized up, he could only flop onto the road. A torrent of blood under pressure hit Sina's apron before she could punch the dressing into the wound. Alfonso screamed.

The paramedics worked swiftly to pack the wound with more and more dressings, making sure they always kept the pressure on. The casualty was put onto a scoop stretcher, then onto the wheeled gurney, with John's assistance. In seconds, the paramedics had loaded Alfonso into the ambulance along with his wife, their rucksacks and poles.

The ambulance screamed off towards Burgos, in a race against time. If the vascular surgeons could repair the artery quickly, Alfonso's leg may be saved.

The road was covered in blood and littered with wrappers from sterile dressings. Drew had got to his feet and was stretching out. John took a carrier bag from the van driver and cleared up the litter. The van driver gave him a handshake. He looked at the bloodied state of Drew and decided that a smile and a wave were preferable, before driving away.

"How are you?" asked Drew.

"I could do with a bloody drink," said John.

"Me too, but not bloody," said Drew, with a grin. "I think we did our good turn for the day here," looking at the blood stains on his arms, legs and clothes. Like day one for an abattoir apprentice, he thought to himself.

They started walking.

"Don't reckon that guy would have survived if you hadn't acted like you did. How did you know what to do?" asked John.

"It's kind of like your blood is in a big sink and it's pouring out of the drain. You've gotta plug it. Simple as that, but it's not nice," Drew said, finding his water bottle to take a good long drink.

"It also helped that when I was in the army I had a girlfriend who was training to be a battlefield medic."

"You need a shower," said John.

"At least one, maybe two," said Drew, relieved that the ordeal was over.

◆ ◆ ◆

After about a kilometre the pilgrims saw a *Guardia Civil* police car heading along the N-120 at speed.

"Act cool John. Don't react. Don't look up," said Drew as he angled himself behind him as the police car flashed by. If the police officers were heading for the dog bite incident and saw Drew covered in blood they would probably stop and start asking awkward questions. The less they engaged with the police the better.

◆ ◆ ◆

In the next village there was a water point. Drew cleaned himself up. Using some liquid soap from his wash kit he got most of the blood from his arms and legs. Traces of dried blood remained stubbornly under his fingernails. This will stop me biting my nails for a while, he thought.

He stripped off and put on a fresh shirt, shorts and socks. Regrettably, the blood-soaked clothes would need to be thrown away. Trying to wash bloodied clothes could cause unwelcome attention. Even with a machine-wash he imagined that the stains would still be visible on his stone-coloured shirt and beige shorts. The discarded clothes represented less weight to be carried. Every cloud has a silver lining.

"Does that trauma bother you?" asked John, sitting in the shade watching Drew washing and re-packing.

"Na, not really. I just try to mentally compartmentalise it," Drew said, with a hand action as if he was throwing something over his shoulder. "It happened. It's in the past. I won't think about it again. I'll just look forward to the future." Drew got out a battered *baguette* sandwich and shared it with John.

"Ooo! Let me guess. Could it be sliced meat and cheese?" said John, with fake enthusiasm.

"How did you know?" said Drew, with mock surprise.

The sandwich was accompanied by a hard-boiled egg and washed down with water, flavoured with salty electrolyte powder.

"What if we bump into the pilgrims I saw today at the scene? What should I say?" asked John.

"Good call," Drew paused, then said. "You're right. We will see them, I'm sure. They're bound to ask you what happened. Just pour a bucket of cold water on it, say it was a 'medical emergency' say you don't know what it was about. Act daft."

"Act daft? *Ja*, I can do that," said John, lifting his rucksack and strapping it on.

"Let's walk," said Drew.

On the way out of the village Drew surreptitiously dropped his bundle of bloodied clothes into a large bin at the cemetery.

❖ ❖ ❖

As arranged, Noel Kavanagh met an undergraduate from the School of Film and Media Arts Cleveland State University at his late father's apartment.

The student had called around to collect video tapes to be used for study and archival purposes. At the bottom of a battered cardboard box was a VHS tape labelled 'Belfast 1983 copy'.

8. BELORADO

It had gone 1 pm by the time the pair walked into Belorado. They passed several *albergues* including the municipal one, each time Drew saying to John, "There may be something a little bit better further on."

They stuck to the yellow arrow route and found the *albergue* Cuatro Cantones. They were almost out of luck as there was only one bed left, but the *hospitalero* was undaunted as he had a solution. The solution turned out to be a mattress on the floor.

Drew and John settled into the dormitory. John took the bed, Drew the mattress.

"Is this what you meant by 'something a little bit better?'" said John, teasing Drew.

The rest of the bunks in the dormitory were taken with a group of four Spanish women, a woman from China and a man from Taiwan.

Drew chuckled when he overheard one of the Spanish women mention, "*Cama para perro*," when referring to his mattress in the corner. He took his wash kit and shuffled off to the shower. Drew noticed that the run-off water was *rosé*-coloured as the last remnants of Alfonso's dried on blood washed away.

Also in the *albergue* was an informal group which Drew labelled The Young Crowd. They were a mixed party in their mid- to late-twenties. Several Germans, a Swede, a few Americans and Canadians and some Brits and Irish.

◆ ◆ ◆

"A Yankees fan all of a sudden?" said Drew pointing at the baseball cap, with a distinctive NY logo, on John's pillow.

"*Ja* I found it on my bed. I think it's Ellen's," said John.

"Do you think she dropped it on your bed by accident?"

"*Ja*. Why else would it be there?"

"Why indeed. Could it have been deliberate? A ruse to get you to chase her maybe?'"

"Now you mention it," said John, uncertainly. "What should I do? Chuck it?"

"Leave it with me. I will give it back to her and have a quiet word."

◆ ◆ ◆

At 4 pm Isabella answered the double knock on the interconnecting hotel door. Juan was dressed in a blouson jacket, shirt and cargo trousers.

"*Bueno*," said Isabella, looking Juan up and down.

"I take direction well," he replied, sheepishly.

"Well you'll be delighted to know that we are

moving in tomorrow to surveil the target. Stop you getting restless. So work out the routes from here to intercept at a place called Tosantos. Take a radio, spray, cuffs and baton, just in case."

"At last, a chance for some action," said Juan, excitedly.

❖ ❖ ❖

The sitrep at 6 pm went well as Drew sat in the awning outside the Kais grill on the Plaza Mayor in Belorado.

Drew explained that John had had some interest from a young American female pilgrim, he said he would have a quiet word with her and tell her her future.

"Who is this woman?" asked Peter, his interest piqued.

"Just a random pilgrim from the East Coast, I think. I'll give her the gypsy's warning and tell her to back off. Why the concern?"

"All celebs, public figures and the mega wealthy have cranks. You know people with, how can I put this delicately 'an incomplete grasp on reality.'" said Peter. "They're 'nucking futs' if you know what I mean?"

"Yes. Like trolls and stalkers?"

"Yeah, that sort of thing. I mean I try to risk assess each contact to figure out if they pose a real threat or they're simply deluded. That's why I'm interested. This woman might not be as 'random' as you think. So keep me posted if there are any developments, okay?"

"Yes, okay. Oh, one more thing."

"Bloody hell, you sound like Lieutenant Columbo, what else have you got for me?" said Peter.

Drew explained that a couple of feral dogs attacked a pilgrim, a Spaniard called Alfonso. John and he gave first aid, they left after the ambulance took the badly injured man away, but before the *Guardia Civil* turned up. There was the possibility though that the incident could get picked up by the local news media.

"You really shouldn't have got involved, but thanks for letting me know. I will put my feelers out," said Peter.

"Yes, well I'm not going to let someone bleed out and die, you heartless sod. Good night," Drew then terminated the call.

◆ ◆ ◆

"Missing your cap?" said Drew to Ellen in the kitchen of Cuatro Cantones.

"Oh my God! Has it been found?" Ellen said, excitedly.

"I guess it was found exactly where you left it. Here it is," Ellen tried to take her cap, but Drew did not release his grip. "Just to let you know I am a bit protective of John. Mentally, he has his demons and is really in need of fresh air and above all else -

solitude."

"Is he some kind of a whack job? Maybe he shouldn't be among decent folk ya know," said Ellen, trying to tug the cap from Drew's grasp.

"He's alright, just had a really crappy time lately. John's working stuff out here on The Way. So please, if you care about the lad, just give him some space," said Drew, allowing Ellen to take her cap.

"How can I help him?" she offered.

"Don't flash your baby blues at him," said Drew, in a no-nonsense way, "and just back right off, honey."

"Are you his bodyguard or something?"

"Bodyguard? How ridiculous," scoffed Drew.

"I'll think about what you said. And that's all I'm saying," then said, "and FYI my name ain't Honey, it's Ellen."

❖ ❖ ❖

At 7.30 pm most pilgrims filed into the restaurant in the *albergue*. Drew and John were seated at a table with Tom, a lawyer from Chicago, and Martin from the Netherlands who worked for the Rotterdam local authority.

"How was that guy?" Tom asked John. "Had he had an accident or something?"

"Oh I don't know. I was just asked to find out if there were any medics amongst you, is all," said John.

"It must have been awful. I mean to escort us

to the far side of the road," said Martin, fishing for more information.

"I'd rather not talk about it," said John, suddenly finding something on his phone of great interest.

Tom persisted, "Dear Lord, the speed that ambulance came past us. Wow! I never knew they could go that fast. Must have been a real life or death situation we reckoned."

"As I said, I'd rather not talk about it. May we change the subject?" said John.

"I fancy the lentil soup then the cod," announced Drew, handing the menu to John.

Whenever the conversation lagged during the meal, Drew would ask his dining companions about when they had first heard about the *Camino de Santiago*, or seek their views on trekking poles, or whether they preferred to use water bottles as opposed to a water bladder system.

The dog bite incident never came up again.

◆ ◆ ◆

After dinner Drew and John had an early night.

Sleep did not come quickly at all. Drew lay awake in the dark on his dog bed mattress. He heard someone move about in bed then climb down the ladder from a top bunk. The pilgrim limped through the dormitory to the bathroom. How can you tell the person had a limp? Drew thought to himself. When someone walks with an injury, or blisters, the sound of footfall is asymmetric and often one foot makes a scuffing noise as it drags. It is strange the little things you pick up on when you share a dormitory with others.

Drew soon realised his mattress was far too close to the bathroom for comfort. He could clearly hear the sound of the toilet roll rotating like the wheel of fortune, or misfortune; and all too clearly the sounds of diarrhoea and vomiting. He cursed whoever made interior walls so thin and blessed whoever made ear plugs.

9. BELORADO TO SAN JUAN

<u>534 km to Santiago de Compostela.</u>

It was early in the morning when something woke Drew. In fact, much too early. There was a very faint but very annoying tapping sound. He checked his watch. Good God! It was not yet 5 am. Someone in the dormitory had not managed to adjust to the jet lag, or the change of time zones and was getting some emailing done. They also had not managed to disable the keyboard sound on their phone. He guessed it was the man from Taiwan.

A fellow Spanish pilgrim was a 'rabbit of negative euphoria' (an unhappy bunny) and expressed her displeasure by shouting, "*Joder*!"

The nocturnal emailer got the message. Silence returned.

◆ ◆ ◆

By 6.30 am Drew had scooped up his kit from around his mattress and quietly left the dormitory. John followed soon after.

In the kitchen area they packed their

rucksacks and got themselves ready. A few of The Young Crowd were also around, grabbing a coffee before they started out.

When the pair were ready Drew whispered, "Let's walk," and they left the *albergue* into the cold pre-dawn of Belorado.

As they were walking John asked, "What was that word the woman shouted this morning? It sounded like "Ho There!""

"Ah yes. *'Joder'* is a very quaint old Spanish way for saying 'fuck,'" said Drew, chuckling.

"Ah, now that makes sense," said John.

They walked mainly in silence until the sun rose and started to take the chill out of the air.

❖ ❖ ❖

"What's up with your feet John?" asked Drew, after watching him walk awkwardly.

"Just a little blister. I'm fine."

With all the happenings over the past few days, Drew had neglected to make sure John was OK. Drew was annoyed with himself. They were due a rest break and for Drew to strip off his windcheater.

"Do you mind if I take a look at your feet?" said Drew, in a tone which implied it was more of an instruction than a polite request.

"Do I have a choice?" asked John, wearily.

"Nope. If you can't go on, I can't go on. So, boots and socks off soldier," said Drew, getting his first aid kit out, just in case, and putting his reading glasses on.

John's heels were the problem. The right heel had an intact blister and the left one had burst, exposing angry red skin about the size of a thumbnail.

"The good news is that your feet are doing really well, John. No blisters underneath or around your toes. The bad news is that both of your heels have issues though, as you must know," said Drew.

"*Ja*, I'm alright," said John. "It's nothing. No problem."

"It will be a problem if the left blister gets infected. The right one may rupture at any time and it also could lead to infection. So I suggest I drain the fluid from the right one and tape it up and clean the left one and put a dressing on it. What do you think?"

John agreed, so Drew got on and tended to his feet.

"Leave the tape on the right one alone. Maybe in a few days in the shower it will come off. Then I can check it, put a little more antiseptic cream on it and strap it up."

"What about the other one?" asked John.

"That's the one I'm worried about. When you shower later, wash it carefully with plenty of soap and water. Rinse and pat it dry, then let me check it."

"Okay dad," said John, cheekily.

"I want to prevent you from getting any more

blisters. Your heel must be moving up and down too much and rubbing as you walk. Try and tighten the laces at the top of your boot to reduce the friction. *Claro?*" said Drew.

"*Claro.*"

◆ ◆ ◆

Drew and John approached a small village called Tosantos.

"Life happens. Coffee helps," said Drew, as he saw Bar Caléndula on the right.

The popular café-bar was run by a friendly young couple. Drew and John took a table outside to enjoy the warmth of the sun. While John relaxed and took off his boots, Drew went inside. He returned with their usual coffees and favourite pastries. Several other outside tables were occupied. The bar was doing well.

Once they were finished, Drew took the crockery back into the bar and they set off again.

◆ ◆ ◆

When the pair got walking Drew said, "Have you read Kipling's book called Kim?"

"Nope," said John, before he asked, "What was it about?"

"Kim was a young lad being trained to be a spy and was shown a tray of objects, maybe a dozen or so and had to memorise them. Then one or more of the items was removed and Kim had to say what had changed."

John decided that it had been foolish to ask Drew what the bloody book was about. There was obviously something bugging him, so he went along with the conversation, "I think I played it at a friend's birthday party when I was about ten. It was a bit lame man."

"Yes, but a good test of observation and recall though."

John had become exasperated, "Okay, that's a minute of my life I'm not going to get back. Is there a point to this or do you just love the sound of your own voice?"

"Describe the customers at that bar we just stopped at."

John mentioned vaguely a group of three pilgrims who were leaving as they arrived. A couple of pilgrims, in a bit more detail, sat at a table having beers and another couple who were sitting drinking coffee.

"Yes, very good. Focus in on the couple drinking coffee. Tell me about them."

"A man and woman. She looked thirty-ish I'd guess, the guy was younger, maybe in his twenties. They had that slightly olive coloured skin and dark hair, typical Spaniards I'd say. Casually dressed, but not pilgrims."

"Good. Why do you say 'not pilgrims?'" asked Drew, pleased with John's deduction.

"Their clothes and footwear looked too clean," said John.

"Okay. How did they interact?"

"They tried to ignore the fact that other customers were around; pretended to be in a bubble. They didn't acknowledge us, or anyone else in fact. So probably not locals."

"Alright, go on."

"She seemed a bit more relaxed, trying to read a guidebook, with her sunglasses on. He was a bit more on edge, fidgety, kept checking his phone and glanced at us a couple of times."

"What do you reckon their relationship was?"

"They seemed a bit uncomfortable, more like an unhappy couple or work colleagues maybe," said John, wondering where this conversation was going.

"Not having an affair then?"

"No. People having an affair seem to have a lot of fun. They would be sitting closer, chatting, laughing, holding hands - mentally undressing each other. He looked rough, like a bouncer from a nightclub. I'd say she was older and classy, out of his league. Ill-matched. Why? What's up?" said John, thinking that there was more to these people than a couple having a coffee at a bar.

"I agree with your observations. They're not a holiday couple and a bit off the beaten track. I wondered how they got to Tosantos," Drew speculated.

"Well they didn't walk there. Their clothes weren't dusty like ours and they didn't have any day pack or water bottles with them," John mused aloud.

"The public transport is a bit sketchy so I presume they arrived by car, but I didn't see one at the café. So maybe they arrived by car and parked it out of sight, then occupied a table before we arrived and stayed until after we left. Smells a bit fishy to me is all."

◆ ◆ ◆

A few minutes after Drew and John left the bar, Isabella and Juan walked back to their car parked outside Bar El Castaño, on the far side of the main road in Tosantos.

"I hoped the targets would just walk past. Bad luck that they stopped at the same café," said Juan.

"It was always a strong possibility. I don't know why I listened to your suggestion to sit outside that place," Isabella said, annoyed with herself. "What did you make of them?"

"Can't believe how vulnerable the young *Chico* is," Juan laughed, "and the *Hombre* is ten years older than God. He couldn't fight sleep!"

"We will report back to the Chief that we have had a close visual on the targets. You must learn to act more naturally. You were like a cat on a hot tin roof. I wouldn't be surprised if we were spotted."

"They were just having a drink and a chat, not a care in the world," said Juan, trying unsuccessfully to reassure Isabella. "With respect, I think you might be a little bit overly anxious."

Isabella seethed and thought, I can't wait to get this contract done, so I don't have to work with this clown anymore. Surely there's a village somewhere missing its idiot.

◆ ◆ ◆

About an hour and a half later Drew and John marched into Villafranca Montes de Oca. They decided it was too early for another break and, after passing the Iglesia de Santiago Apóstol, the path got steeper, and steeper still.

For an hour The Way zig-zagged uphill and both pilgrims stopped talking as they dug deep into their reserves of energy to haul themselves along. Eventually they reached the Monumento La Pedraja at the top.

"*Ag*, that was a bastard *bergie*," complained John, about the climb.

Drew agreed.

10. SAN JUAN DE ORTEGA

After their long uphill slog to Alto de la Pedraja and an hour or so of walking through a forest the men were keen to take a break. As they entered the village of San Juan de Ortega, John was tempted by a busy looking bar on the left.

"It's not always a good idea to go to the first bar you see. Let's carry on through the village and try to find somewhere else," said Drew.

"That place looked fine to me. How do you know there actually will be something else?" asked John, keen to stop and rest his feet.

"I've just seen a sign for another bar."

The bar La Cuadra de Luisito looked like an ideal place to take a break, have a well-earned beer and check John's feet, before continuing to Agés or Atapuerca. Drew went inside the bar, while John sat outside enjoying the sunshine.

A few minutes later, Drew emerged with a couple of beers and a proposal, "If it's all the same with you we will stay here tonight. There's an *albergue* above the bar and, as luck would have it, they have two beds left."

John handed Drew his passport and *credential*

as he sipped his beer, smiled and said, "The *Camino* does indeed provide."

◆ ◆ ◆

After the men had showered, settled in and taken their customary afternoon snooze, Drew found a discreet table outside the *albergue* and settled down to take the sitrep video call at 6 pm.

"Dixie, *hola que tal*?" said Drew.

"Oh, your *Afrikaans* is coming along beautifully matey," said Peter, playfully. "How's tricks?"

Drew briefed Peter about the past 24 hours. Ellen, the chatty American, had been asked to back off. The walking had been tough, but uneventful. He decided not to mention the fact that John had acquired a brace of blisters.

"That's it from us. You got anything?" asked Drew.

"Nope. Nothing to report on the media front about that dog bite. Maybe it was not newsworthy, just a nip perhaps," said Peter.

Some 'nip' thought Drew, "Oh we did see a couple this morning who looked a bit... out of place. Odd, you know?"

"Where was that?" asked Peter.

"Hang on, lemme think... Oh yeah, a small village called Tosantos. Just a tuppenny-ha'penny place, blink and you'd miss it. Just as we got to the village, there's this little bar with a few pilgrims.

We stopped and there was this strange looking couple outside having coffee," said Drew, trying to remember as much about them as he could.

"What were they like?" asked Peter.

"I bloody knew you'd ask me that," said Drew, as he went on to describe them in as much detail as he could recall.

"What spiked your senses?" said Peter, scribbling a few notes.

"The village was well off the beaten track, not a tourist hotspot, and they interacted more like employees than as a couple. The woman was tidy, a 'looker' you might say. I reckon the man could handle himself, a bit of a bruiser. If he was in a relationship with the woman he was definitely 'punching above his weight.'"

"Did you clock a vehicle?" asked Peter.

"No, sorry."

"Too much to ask if you snatched a cheeky photo of them?"

"Er... I refer you to the answer I gave a few moments ago."

"Ah well. Probably nothing to worry about. Apart from that, any scandal, gossip, rumour, or...?" asked Peter.

"Smut? Nope. We should be in Burgos tomorrow. Bye then," said Drew.

"Enjoy the bright lights of Burgos when you get there matey. Cheers," said Peter, who then disconnected.

◆ ◆ ◆

The bar staff promised a delicious communal meal for the pilgrims of homemade pumpkin soup, bread, *paella* with salad followed by a dessert. All washed down with jugs of local red wine.

What Drew and John were not promised was a latecomer and larger-than-life character to sit at the end of the table between them.

"Ah good evening to you boys. I'm Seán from County Donegal. Red wine for ya?" said the newcomer. Drew declined the red wine; John did not.

"Hey! That hill outta Villafranca today was a *fecker* right enough. *Jeezo* enough to give a man a thirst, so it did. *Slàinte!*" as Seán saluted John with a glass of wine, before draining it in a single gulp.

Seán had a seemingly limitless store of tall tales and jokes at the expense of an unnamed and hapless man from County Kerry.

Seán and John emptied the first wine jug before they had finished the *paella*. As a second jug appeared, courtesy of a group of abstemious American pilgrims at the far end of the table, John greeted it with a cheery, "The *Camino* provides!"

Drew's spirits sank as he saw John's efforts to keep up the pace of Seán's thirst quenching. John was reluctant to take the hint from Drew that he should slow down. He tried to signal to him to stop drinking wine by sliding a glass of water to him. Seán saw the gesture and declared with a hearty laugh, "Don't drink it John. Fish piss in it!"

The staff encouraged the pilgrims to leave the tables so that the locals could be fed. Most took this as their cue to head off to bed. Not so Seán and his new drinking buddy. Seán went over to the bar and began regaling John with accounts of his numerous amorous conquests, "I've never been to bed with an ugly woman," he announced, "but I have woken up with a few."

Back in the dormitory Drew made sure his phone and head torch were recharging. The other pilgrims got on with catching up on messaging family and friends, updating journals or blogs, personal hygiene needs and sorting their kit so they could get away quietly in the morning.

Quiet was not the order of the day from the bar underneath the dormitory as the drinkers became increasingly drunk. At one point Drew heard Seán say loudly, "Ah, will you not have a *wee* brandy? Ah, go on."

❖ ❖ ❖

At 10 pm the dormitory lights were switched off and two heavily inebriated pilgrims stumbled in. With lots of slurred whispers Seán and John found their respective bunks.

John climbed into his top bunk where he had left a heavy bag with clothes, sandals and washing kit. In his drunken attempt to carefully lower the bag to the floor, he dropped it with a resounding thud.

A minute later Seán said, "Ah *jeezo* John! Will you drop the other boot and let us get to *feckin'* sleep!" The witty remark produced a few giggles in the dark.

Sometime later Seán said, "Are you alright there John?"

"Uh huh," muttered John.

"Ah! That's grand. So it is."

A bit later Seán slurred, "John. Are you sure you're alright?"

John responded sleepily, "Ah hah."

Someone in the darkness uttered, "Shhhh!"

"Ah, get to *feck!*" responded Seán.

An unknown female shouted, "*Puta!*"

Seán, with a lack of understanding of Spanish swear words and the limitations of human anatomy, replied, "Ah! Stick your hooter up your pooter."

The talking stopped.

The snoring began.

Drew sighed and reached for his ear plugs.

11. SAN JUAN TO BURGOS

<u>510 km to Santiago de Compostela.</u>

"Up and at 'em John," said Drew. It was past 6.30 am, most pilgrims were up and getting ready to go. Drew was impatient to be off.

John yawned and stretched in his bunk, "Ah dad! I'll look for a job tomorrow."

"Don't piss me about. It's time we were on our way."

"What's the rush?" asked John.

John had started to test Drew's patience.

"Well Burgos is likely to be busy and if you don't fancy sleeping on a park bench with the winos, I suggest you get your bag of bones out of bed, get your boots on... Hey, you know the drill. Get movin' will you?"

"You go on, old timer. I'll easily catch you up," said John, before rolling on his side away from Drew. For a minute Drew thought of introducing John to Aesop's fable of the tortoise and the hare, but decided it was not worth it. Back in his military days he would be reminding the reluctant soldier of the army rank structure, with lots of profanity and violent imagery.

Instead Drew said, "That works for me John. *Buen* bloody *Camino*." He left the dormitory, making sure he had all of his kit. Drew stepped out into the cold and dark.

The sky was cloudless with a multitude of stars. Soon The Way veered off the road and onto a forest track.

As he walked alone in the dark, Drew felt a mixture of confidence and exasperation with his protégé. He reflected on John's progress. When he met him in Logroño he did not think he would last the day. After Nájera, John wanted to quit, but he just kept on going. Drew was grateful for John's help at the dog bite incident before Belorado. He had stepped up to the plate, so to speak. John had understood about Ellen's unwanted advance and the implications for his rehabilitation. John had clocked the suspicious couple outside the bar at Tosantos. His security awareness was developing well. Even though John was suffering from blistered feet, he put in the distance and attacked the hills.

Drew was annoyed that John gave into the peer pressure from Seán and got drunk. He was, however, confident that John could make his own way that morning. Drew would wait at the first watering hole and give him an hour to catch up.

◆ ◆ ◆

The San Rafael bar at Agés looked warm and inviting, Drew approached the counter and the proprietor told him to go back out and leave his backpack in the hallway. On re-entering the bar, Drew ordered a *cortado* and *tortilla*.

Drew dug out a sachet of *sambal* from his rucksack to spice up the *tortilla*. The starchy warm *tortilla* of potatoes and onions fried in olive oil, enriched with eggs and garlic was enlivened with the hot sauce.

Before Drew finished his coffee, Seán entered the bar wearing his rucksack. After getting told off by the proprietor, he too came back without it. He ordered a coffee and a *croissant*.

"Morning Seán. Seen John on your travels?"

"Are you worried about his whereabouts?" said Seán in an amusing phraseology which only he could pull off.

"Yes, you could say I am 'worried about his whereabouts,'" said Drew with a smile.

"Ah, he'll be along presently, so he will. He was getting ready as I left. I will have to get going," Seán explained that he was not stopping in Burgos and was heading home after meeting a friend in Tardajos.

"I always say, the best lunches always starts at one o'clock and finish in Donegal a week later." With that he downed his coffee and pastry before leaving.

Drew's phone pinged. A cryptic SMS message from Dixie:

Watch out. Speak at 6

Drew was puzzled and worried. He now really regretted leaving John on his own.

Drew was relieved when John turned up a few minutes later looking subdued, "Sorry, Drew." His face had a slight grey-green tinge, rather than his usual fresh complexion.

"John, I'm a very old dog and I don't like getting pissed about by young pups," said Drew, tersely. "So here it is. Bit by bit you are getting more freedom to choose what you want to do. If you want to drink your bodyweight in booze with your new mate Seán. Fine. But I'm not making allowances for you. Time to grow up."

"*Ja*. Message received," muttered John.

"Good. Lecture over," said Drew, before changing his tone to a more friendly one, "And now, what do you want for breakfast? A coffee and a sticky bun?"

"Thanks, but I think it's about time I started ordering for myself," said John, as he walked slowly to the counter.

John returned shakily with a *café con leche grande* and a *croissant*. The barman called to Drew, "*Noches alegres, mañanas tristes!*" and laughed. Drew nodded.

"Let me guess. I take it that comment was at my expense," said John.

"Yes," Drew nodded. "The barman said 'a happy

night is followed by a sad morning' or something like that."

Once John had eaten and returned his crockery to the bar he left with Drew.

❖ ❖ ❖

The Way was fairly flat from Agés to Atapuerca, but the hill up to Matagrande was an unforgiving bastard.

Drew kept going, adjusting his speed and stride to the hill. Keeping a steady mile-munching pace going. Using his trekking pole, he passed other pilgrims as they kept on slowing down and stopping. Drew coordinated his breathing with the tempo of his pace.

John tried to keep up with the old man. He got mental visions of hopeless despair and a feeling of impending doom. His mind sabotaged his body's efforts. John's stomach, still with its residual red wine, found the addition of milky coffee an insult and he was sick - lavishly.

❖ ❖ ❖

Eventually, John got to the summit where Drew was waiting for him to enjoy the dawn. Drew had waited so long, in fact, that he had time to put on a fleece top to prevent himself getting chilled. It was true to say that John did not quite share Drew's enthusiasm for the aesthetic beauty of the sunrise.

They pushed on and went down the hill, with the city of Burgos in the far distance, set in endless arable land. John was in purgatory with the dehydration of a hangover, the exertion of climbing Matagrande and trying to keep up with Drew. He lagged behind.

◆ ◆ ◆

After Orbaneja Riopico they crossed the road bridge and Drew saw pilgrims heading left, whereas the official *Camino* sign definitely pointed straight ahead.

"What do you reckon we should do John?"

"Er, check the app?" suggested John.

Drew turned around and looked at a man and a young woman following them. He shrugged his shoulders and raised his arms. The woman pointed down the unmarked track on the left.

"Why are we not taking the proper Way?" asked John.

"I read that the original path, which led to the river, was hard to find and the new route went through the industrial outskirts," said Drew, he pointed at a worn out painted yellow arrow on the road, not immediately visible, "Looks like we have found the Old Way."

◆ ◆ ◆

Drew and John walked around the boundary fence of Burgos airport and passed a field of sunflowers.

"What do you see in the field?" asked Drew.

"A man walking through the sunflowers," said John.

"And..."

"Oh, there's a dog in front of him. It's sniffing around and sweeping either side."

"And..."

"Oh, *kak*. The guy's got a gun," John said, with a little concern.

"Very good. What sort of gun?" Drew asked, calmly.

"Looks like a shotgun. It's down at his side, horizontal."

"Okay. What don't you see?"

"Getting tired of this Drew. *Ag*, spit it out, man."

Drew explained that John had identified a hazard, the shotgun. Had figured out that the man was out hunting in the fields for birds or rabbits. There were no others with him and no vehicle, so the risk he posed to John was low.

"So, unless you're a shapeshifter and become a tweety bird or a bunny you shouldn't come to any harm. I'm just very pleased with your personal sense of security. This morning I wasn't concerned about you being left on your own."

"Is that a vote of confidence in me?" asked John.

"Yeah. I reckon so. By the way, are you feeling any better?"

"*Ja.* A hell of a lot better than before. At last my *babelaas* is wearing off. I thought I was dying," replied John, teaching Drew the *Afrikaaner* word for a hangover.

◆ ◆ ◆

The riverside route into Burgos was painfully long.

"Why do the last couple of kilometres of the day feel like fifty?" complained John.

"Ha. I've often wondered that myself," replied Drew, looking up ahead to the footbridge which would take them finally into the heart of the city.

"Damn it. Let's sit down on this wall," said Drew quickly. John was puzzled. It was not far to go until they got to the end of the day's walk. Something was wrong.

"What's up?" said John.

Drew calmly got out his water bottle, "Don't react to what I'm going to say. About a hundred metres ahead there is a news TV van parked next to the footbridge where we will have to pass to get into town."

"Okay. I see it," said John, puzzled.

"There are a couple of people sitting in camping chairs outside. I'm not sure but it looks like Alfonso's wife and I presume the other person is a journalist. I guess they've figured out that we will pass here this afternoon and are going to interview us for their 'dog bites man' story."

"*Kak*. Can we go back?" asked John.

"We could, but it would look suspicious to the journalist who may scent an even juicier story and it would look odd to all of the pilgrims coming the other way," said Drew, trying to figure a way of getting past Alfonso's wife without her spotting them. A solution materialised.

A large group of Spanish pilgrims came along the path. In anticipation of getting to the end of the day they were animated, talking loudly.

As the Spaniards passed them with happy, "*Buen Camino*," greetings the pair joined the group.

"Keep on the right, away from the TV van, hood up, keep your head down and don't look over at Alfonso's wife," said Drew, as they walked along with the crowd.

"What if we get spotted?" asked John.

"Just follow me. I will try to outpace them and shout '*los baños*,'" said Drew, hoping that even an intrepid journalist would not wish to chase someone in a rush to the toilets. Drew and John held their breath as they passed the van, using the Spaniards as cover.

When they reached the footbridge, the Spaniards decided to take a break.

"Just keep going," Drew whispered to John and they sped up as they crossed into Burgos. Instead of turning around, Drew used the reflection in the windows of the offices ahead to see that they were not being followed.

"Phew that was close. Do you think they will

try again?" asked John.

"Maybe," said Drew, "but today's newspaper is tomorrow's chip wrapper, so I guess that the media organisation will have other stories to cover and the wife would rather be with Alfonso than wasting her time. We will just need to keep our eyes peeled."

12. BURGOS

The impressive cathedral in Burgos was busy hosting a wedding when the men arrived in the city after their long approach beside the river.

The anxiety of not finding a bed for the night spurred Drew on to the Casa del Cubo de Burgos. There seemed to be no shortage of beds and the pair settled into the shared dormitory with most of The Young Crowd.

Once Drew had showered, he collected the washing and headed for the laundry room. The single washing-machine had a few minutes left so Drew waited for it to finish its cycle.

The young Italian *peregrina*, who had indicated the river route approach to Burgos, looked distraught as she arrived with her bundle of laundry. Drew offered to combine their clothes into one load to save time and money.

The Italian took charge of the process from washing-machine to tumble dryer and once completed, separated her clothes from Drew and John's. This saved Drew the awkwardness of handling the petite young Italian's lingerie.

While Drew was waiting for his clothes to dry, he was joined by Siobhán, an engineer from Ireland and a core member of The Young Crowd.

She lamented the fact that her underwear kept on going astray in the laundry process.

"I'm sure my knickers are *feckin'* cursed," she said.

"Maybe you can get them exorcised when you get to Santiago."

"Ah yes. God bless these knickers," said Siobhán, laughing.

"...and all those who enter them."

"Cheeky old sod," Siobhán said, rebuking Drew.

Drew took his washing to the dormitory and handed John his freshly cleaned clothes.

"Have you checked your blisters?"

"*Ja*. I've washed and dried my feet. No new ones. The two on the heels are okay," said John.

Drew checked John's blisters and re-dressed them.

❖ ❖ ❖

The cryptic message 'Watch out' from Peter had rattled Drew. So far, the *Camino* had just been uneventful, apart from nearly being ambushed by Mrs Alfonso and a journalist on the way into the city. He had warned-off Ellen and seen a strange couple in Tosantos, but apart from that there had been no security issues he was aware of. The only thing John had to worry about so far was himself and his tendency to want to get steaming drunk. They had come to a decent working arrangement, more or less. What have I missed? thought Drew.

With a little trepidation, Drew initiated the video meeting. It was answered immediately by Peter, who appeared to be in a corporate office, "Hello matey. How's everything?"

"Fine Dixie. Your message spooked me. What's up?"

"Just getting the jungle drums beating on social media about John. Have you noticed any paparazzi or anything like that recently?" said Peter.

"Funny you should mention that. Just as we were walking into Burgos, I spotted Alfonso's wife with a news crew van which I reckoned was from a local media outlet. I think they were trying to spot us to do an interview. Apart from that nothing."

"Apart from nearly getting ambushed by a TV crew? That's not nothing matey," said Peter. "We were aware that the dog bite incident has caused a bit of a stir. The local online media are running with a 'Devil Dog' story. You'll be relieved to hear that the victim survived by the skin of his teeth. The woman recalled the horror of the attack, all hyped up by the journos of course. She thanked the unknown Good Samaritans who gave Alfonso first aid. She described her helper as looking like a blonde Jesus, with dancing blue eyes. I guess she was talking about John rather than you."

"Yes I reckon she was," said Drew. "Hope the media interest will blow over in a day or two."

"Me too. Where's a good old political sex scandal when you need one eh," said Peter. "Oh yeah, before I forget, the local media newsline has put out a plea for anyone who knows the identity of the first aiders to email them. So they may try again to contact you."

"Okay. Anyway what was behind your message to me this morning then?" asked Drew

"Oh yeah. We have software which has picked up interest in John linked to the *Camino*. Our social media experts are getting really twitchy. It could be that John's face has appeared on a pilgrim photo which has spiked interest."

"What do you think may happen next?"

"You could get the paps being all ballsy and trying to confront him like today, or it could be more subtle. Maybe a clandestine approach. Anyhow forewarned is forearmed and all that bullshit," said Peter, trying to be upbeat about the situation.

"Would it be so bad if John is filmed being on a pilgrimage anyway?"

"Er, damn right it would," said Peter. "His only security is his anonymity. As soon as his cover is blown, he is out of there, matey. Make sure you keep your wits about you. Can you think of any occasion when he might have been snapped?"

"I mean there are cameras everywhere Dixie, you know that. Everyone with a bloody phone has got a camera for God's sake. Then there's CCTV and doorbell cameras. John has been good at keeping his baseball cap on. There was this one time though," Drew paused. "Yes, a few nights back at a place called **Santo Domingo**, we had a meal in the *albergue* and John was in a selfie with an Italian couple, but hell it could have been anytime."

"And you didn't stop it?" said Peter, incredulously.

"Dixie, I can't be at his side twenty four hours a day," Drew said, defensively.

"Yep okay, it's the way the world is these days. Everytime I open my fridge and the light comes on I smile as I think I'm having my bloody photo taken. Anyway our analysts will keep on doing their stuff and if they get any solid information I will let you know. In the meantime-"

"Stay vigilant?"

"I was going to say that," said Peter.

"Fat lot of good that is. I don't know what type of threat I'm meant to be looking out for - an assassination, a bleeding kidnapping, a frigging kissogram-"

"Yeah. Whatever matey. You have my permission to get on and cope," said Peter interrupting.

"Thanks a bloody lot," replied Drew, "and good night."

◆ ◆ ◆

At 8 pm Drew and John shuffled into Restaurante El Mítico on the Plaza Mayor.

The day had started badly for both of them, thanks to the previous night's drinking excess.

They had been annoyed with each other, but had come to an understanding. It was as if someone had hit a reset button on their relationship. The tension which had built up between them since they met at Logroño had evaporated. They were having a fresh start.

The pair chose a salad of wild herbs, green shoots, *jamón ibérico*, walnuts and *pâté*. They wisely declined the wine list in favour of sparkling water.

"We may have trouble," said Drew.

"Where?" said John, looking around quickly.

"Not here. Well at least I don't think so anyway. Peter has told me that there is a connection on social media linking you being on the *Camino*."

"Oh, *kak*. What kind of trouble are you thinking about?" asked John.

Drew went through the types of threats from kidnappers to journalists to stalkers, and what they should do.

"So keep your wits about you. Remember we both need to look out for each other. Okay?"

"*Ja*. Okay partner."

Next came a seafood course of grilled scallops and prawns. For his main course Drew chose the grilled sea bass with baked potatoes; whilst John ordered the Sirloin Tataki steak with chips.

The pair discussed the route for the following day.

For dessert they both had *tarta de Santiago*. A moist cake with a good balance of sweetness and almonds. Drew settled the bill in cash.

◆ ◆ ◆

As Drew and John left the restaurant they were being watched.

Across the plaza two brothers eyed the pilgrims with keen interest. Diego was the older and more cautious of the two; Matias his younger, more impetuous sibling.

Drew and John looked like well-off tourists or pilgrims, who were probably carrying passports, phones and bundles of *euros*. The brothers both crushed their cigarettes on the floor and walked briskly across the deserted square.

"Don't look now John, but I think we have trouble. When we get in the side street, you go on ahead and don't wait for me," said Drew, in a calm manner.

When Drew first clapped eyes on the two brothers, he noticed that they both threw away their cigarettes simultaneously. Red flag number one, it was strange to both finish their smokes at exactly the same moment. It was as if they were 'clearing their decks for action.' Red flag number two was them setting off walking quickly across the plaza to intercept them.

John went into the deserted side street first, Drew followed. Part way up the street, construction work fencing had reduced the width to less than two metres. Good, thought Drew, I can deal with the pair one at a time if I have to, in this choke point. They probably have not learnt to fight together, like a team. Hopefully, it won't come to that.

Drew heard the footsteps quicken behind him. "*Hola amigo*," said Matias.

Drew turned and saw the two young men as expected, Matias in front with Diego following up closely behind. There was a light in the street which favoured Drew, it was behind him shining into the brothers' faces. John continued walking.

Drew shrugged and gave a non-threatening open-handed gesture. He was not going to say anything unless he had to.

Matias closed in on Drew and, clicking his fingers, demanded, "*Teléfono! Pasaporte! Dinero!*"

Drew remained motionless until the young man was an arms' length away, then he thumped both his palms into Matias' shoulders to shove him smartly backwards. The young man was caught by surprise and he rocked back into Diego. Diego pushed his brother forwards. Matias had been embarrassed in front of his older brother. He was eager to settle this and teach this old man some manners.

"*Bastardo*," said Matias. Drew stayed silent, took a step to the rear and kept his open palms facing forwards.

Having watched countless martial arts films, Matias had perfected a spinning kick. Firstly, against static punch bags in the gym, then in the ring against sparring partners. He would enjoy delivering a kick to this old man's guts. Matias' mistake was to telegraph his intentions by taking a target glance at Drew's stomach, before springing up and down a couple of times on his left foot.

Drew had seen this move plenty of times and knew that just for a fraction of a second Matias would have to turn his back on him. A few milliseconds perhaps. That was all the time Drew needed.

Matias raised his right leg in the air and started his spin. He would come around and the heel of his right foot would drive deep into Drew's abdomen. Once floored, he would stomp his face into an unrecognisable pulp. Matias had thought too many steps ahead. He also had the overconfidence of youth.

The instant Matias was committed to his spin, Drew closed the one metre gap in a flash. He gripped the lad's shoulders and threw all his weight behind a driving knee strike to the base of Matias' spine, lifting him into the air and fracturing his coccyx. Matias shrieked in agony and fell in a heap on the floor. Drew took a few more steps back. One down, he thought.

Diego had not seen exactly what had happened to his brother, but the old man was still standing there, his arms outstretched, his palms empty. Diego stepped over his brother who was screaming in pain. He shook his head and said, "*No envíes a un niño a hacer el trabajo de un hombre.*" He would show his kid brother how things should be done. Old school style.

Drew was still standing and looked every inch like one of the soft old men Diego had mugged countless times before. Diego walked like an animal moving in for the kill. He balled his hands into fists.

Oh no! thought Drew. A boxer!

Drew always rated boxers as the worst opponents in a street fight. A boxer's mind is not crowded with all manner of martial arts techniques - he only had one technique, the punch. Diego had trained for years to throw combinations of punches and take hits.

A boxer's Achilles heel though was their competitive spirit. A boxer is conditioned to fight another boxer. Drew had seen one tactic work many years back in a barrack room brawl. This was his only chance, it was all or nothing.

Diego thought that he would thrash this old man for hurting his brother and thereby insulting his family's honour. Drew then surprised Diego; he also adopted an orthodox boxer's stance. Feet shoulder width apart, left leg leading, left fist protecting his face, ready to jab and right fist held back to deliver a showstopper blow.

A giant grin appeared on Diego's face. A bit of sport, plus the satisfaction of beating the old bastard senseless in a bare-knuckle contest. Due to the narrowness of the street, Diego could only advance straight at Drew. No chance to use his fancy footwork. Diego was ready to give a demonstration of jabs, hooks and a *coup de grâce* uppercut. With the light shining in his eyes, he failed to see Drew's balance shift to his backfoot.

Drew kept his fists up as he swung his left foot with all his might and connected with full force into Diego's balls. The searing pain took Diego's breath away, he doubled up. Drew moved in and kneed him in the face, smashing his nose and knocking him unconscious. Diego dropped like a stone, flat on his front. Two down.

Drew arranged Diego into the recovery position and made sure his airway was not obstructed. He checked his pulse; strong and regular, if a bit fast. A wallet was sticking out of the back pocket of Diego's jeans. Drew removed the identification card by the edges, to avoid leaving his fingerprints, and photographed it. He slid the wallet and contents back into the pocket.

From the whimpering he knew that Matias would survive, although walking, sitting and crapping would be a whole new world of pain for the next few weeks.

Drew decided that they were probably a pair of opportunist muggers, rather than professional kidnappers. He had heard it said that, 'If it looks like a duck, walks like a duck and quacks like a duck. It's probably a duck.' The brothers only spoke in Spanish to him, maybe if they knew that Drew and John were English-speakers they would have spoken in English. Yes, these two would-be muggers were just a pair of overconfident local punks.

Even so, he could not just leave them. They needed medical help. If they deteriorated it could lead to a major police investigation, which could compromise his mission. Drew could not exactly ring the emergency services. He looked around the quiet street and found the answer.

Drew stood with his back against the wooden delivery doors to the high end *boutique* for ladies *haute couture* fashion and gave it an almighty back kick. On his fourth 'donkey kick' he heard the internal burglar alarm sound. Job done.

He walked casually away, before the police arrived to find two of their most prolific criminals lying flat out. He guessed they would probably have 'frequent flyer' status back in the local police holding cells.

◆ ◆ ◆

At the first corner in the street Drew met John. "Thought I told you to go back to the *albergue*," said Drew.

"Can't believe what I saw. It was amazing! You gave them a *poesklap*, I mean a proper bitch-slap, man," said John, in an excited state after witnessing a masterclass of self-defence techniques.

"Just act naturally, as if nothing has happened," said Drew, walking away slowly. "It didn't have to be that way. They could have backed off. I just got lucky is all. I can't be lucky all the time."

"Will they come after us?" said John.

"Possibly, but I imagine for the next week they will be licking their wounds."

"You never even used your fists, man. Where did you learn to scrap like that?"

"I was taught in the Army to only use my fists once my feet were bleeding," said Drew, jokingly.

"In the boxing ring?" asked John.

"No, usually in the NAAFI," said Drew, with a grin.

"Ah well, it will give you something to tell Uncle Pete about on your next catchup," said John.

"Yes, I'll enjoy telling him all about it and give him something to worry about. Why should he be happy all his life eh?"

◆ ◆ ◆

As they approached the front door of their *albergue* they had to wait for a *Policía Local* van to rush past with its blue lights flashing and siren sounding.

Drew looked at John and shrugged, "Must be an alarm going off somewhere."

"Could be," said John. "Do you think an early start tomorrow might be wise?"

"Definitely. Alarm at six. On The Way by six thirty," said Drew.

Before Drew went into the dormitory he emailed the photograph of Diego's identification card to Peter Dickinson with a message, "Bumped into this chap."

John went into the communal kitchen and found that The Young Crowd were having a bring your own pizza and booze party. He was invited to join the fun, but showed remarkable restraint by politely refusing. The party went on without him.

And on.

And on.

13. BURGOS TO HORNILLOS

<u>484 km to Santiago de Compostela.</u>

As planned, Drew and John were up and ready to be on their way by 6.30 am. In the kitchen of the hostel they saw the aftermath of the party. Bins overflowing with pizza boxes, counters full of empty bottles of rum and coke.

The kitchen tables had all been moved to the side of the room and the chairs arranged in a circle.

"What went on here? A meeting of alcoholics anonymous?" asked John, humorously.

"Maybe. Here are a couple of alcohol-free rum bottles," said Drew, holding up two empty bottles.

"I think we should get going before the *hospitalera* sees this and hits the roof," said John.

❖ ❖ ❖

In Burgos the cleaners were busy jet-washing the dark streets and clearing up the rubbish from the previous night's festivities.

A small coffee shop was open, doing a brisk trade. Drew sat outside with the rucksacks whilst John went in to buy the breakfast items of choice for them both; a *cortado* and *Neapolitana* for Drew, a *café con leche grande* and *croissant* for John.

They ate in silence. As they were finishing John asked, "Will the youngsters get into trouble for the mess in the kitchen?"

"Quite possibly, but the *albergue* is not exclusively for pilgrims. We've been in those places where from ten o'clock it's lights out and silence. Last night's place was open to all, so this must have happened before. All that being said, I'm glad we made an early start," said Drew. "Thanks for breakfast. Let's walk."

◆ ◆ ◆

The men followed the scallop shells set into the pavement. As they left the city centre the scallop shells petered out. There were, however, pilgrims ahead of them to show them The Way.

As usual, following the *Camino* through a city proved difficult. At one point there was a solitary yellow arrow spray painted on a building to indicate a sharp left turn. If they had missed it it could have been a time-consuming process to get back on track. The *Camino* crossed a river and led to a wide main road. A yellow arrow marker clearly pointed to the left hand side of the road, but the pilgrims ahead went to the right instead.

"Hey, I think we should actually go on the left side of the road here Drew, not follow these *mamparas*," said John.

"I hear you, John," said Drew, "but let's not stand out from the crowd. We'll go along with these plonkers and hope the signed route joins us at the next roundabout." Which it did.

The two men discussed The Young Crowd. At first they thought the group were simply on *Camino* as an alternative to cavorting in the night clubs of Ibiza.

"Or maybe they are inspired by the Holy Spirit and are bringing a youthful exuberance to The Way," offered Drew.

"Well they certainly liven things up for sure," said John, with a smile.

"Of course they could be a flash back to the pagan traditions before the Christians monopolised the pilgrimage business."

"Well I'm always pleased to see them. They appear to be having so much fun."

"Yes, and whenever they enter a dormitory they reduce everyone's average age by about thirty years," said Drew, happily.

◆ ◆ ◆

Drew approached Tardajos and scanned around in case Seán from County Donegal was still in town. Not wishing to tempt fate, Drew decided not to stop in any bar, but to keep on going.

As they were heading out of the town all of the routes were marked with a yellow 'X'. It did not seem to make any sense, unless it was to divert bewildered pilgrims into the *albergue* nearby to ask for directions and maybe make a purchase.

"Well this has got me stumped. All of the options have a yellow X. So where the heck is The Way?" said a confused John.

At that moment a local old man was leaving his house to get into a car. Drew caught his eye and raised his arms in a gesture of despair.

"*Directo. Directo*," the local said, pointing straight ahead.

With a wave of thanks the pair continued. *Directo*.

"Do you think he was sent from above?" asked John.

"If you believe he was, then 'yes.'"

◆ ◆ ◆

As they walked along, Drew had heard the occasional loud bang that morning. This was no surprise as they were in farming country and there were hunters and bird scaring devices.

In Rabe de las Calzadas there was an almighty explosion overhead from a firework and as they got to the main square a large group of young people, wearing identical purple sweatshirts, were partying. A bagpipe was playing and people were being offered drink from wine skins.

Long after Drew and John had left the village, they could hear fireworks every few minutes. Whatever the party was in honour of was unclear.

No chance of a lie-in that day in Rabe de las Calzadas.

◆ ◆ ◆

At their next break John asked, "Do you want to tell me about your self-defence techniques, oh great *sensei*?"

"I suppose the best technique is to avoid a confrontation in the first place," replied Drew.

He explained that he would use awareness and try to not get into situations where he would have to fight. If he was confronted he would try and back off and appear to be as non-threatening as possible.

"*Ja*, but sometimes you've gotta fight."

"And these days I haven't got the strength or stamina to scrap for more than a few seconds. So I need to take decisive action. It's not like in the movies where fight scenes go on for ages. Okay, let's walk."

◆ ◆ ◆

On the approach to Hornillos, Drew was joined by a jovial pilgrim from South Korea, called Chen. John was dawdling behind, as usual.

As Chen walked alongside Drew he asked, "Why you doing *Camino*?"

Drew was considering his response and suddenly said, "Oh, do go on ahead, Chen. I've gotta take a leak."

Chen was slightly perplexed as there were no toilets in sight, just lots of bushes, "It okay. I wait you."

Drew's tone was insistent, "No. You go on," as he walked off towards a large shrub.

Confused, Chen walked on.

John caught up with Drew, "Anything wrong?"

"Thought that guy was just having a friendly chat as we were walking along, until I noticed he was filming me," said Drew, keeping a lookout to make sure Chen was not hanging on for him.

"Really?" said John.

"Yeah. He had a video camera on his shoulder strap and was recording me. I don't think he is a hostile. It's maybe just a cultural thing."

"In what way 'cultural?'" asked John.

"He may have felt embarrassed to ask permission to film me."

"Maybe from his country everyone films bloody everything. Welcome to the twenty-first century *Ouballie*," said John, with a smile.

"Suppose you're right. I don't have a problem with someone filming me so they can improve their English, but I don't know the guy and haven't got a Scooby where the footage will end up."

"What do you mean 'Scooby?'" asked John.

"It's rhyming slang. Scooby-Doo rhymes with 'clue.'"

John laughed, "No chance he would have learned anything of your so-called King's English from you!"

14. HORNILLOS DEL CAMINO

The two men got into Hornillos del Camino just before the municipal *albergue* opened at midday. The *hospitalera* allocated them a bunk bed in one of the dormitories. They were told that there was a pilgrim blessing after the 7 pm mass at the church next door. The town quickly filled up and by mid-afternoon the local taxis were doing a roaring trade taking pilgrims onwards, or backwards, to alternative places where they could find lodgings. Hornillos was full. *Completo.*

◆ ◆ ◆

After Drew and John had sorted out their kit, they took a stroll along the road which ran through Hornillos.

As they got towards the end of town a voice from behind them said, "Well John de Witt, what have you got to say to the victims of the mercenaries your father's company deployed in the *Sahel*?"

Drew and John both spun around to see a young man with a GoPro camera and a fluffy microphone on a stick.

John said, "What's this? Some sort of joke eh?"

"This is no joke when women and children are brutalised by your company's mercenaries," said the young man, still pointing his camera and slightly shaky microphone at John.

Drew sidled up to the young man and calmly asked, "Which media outfit do you work for?"

"Answer the question Mr de Witt. Your company has caused untold misery and the public have a right to know how you feel about it," continued the young man.

"Who is your editor?" Drew asked calmly.

John was riled and demanded, "Who the *fok* are you?"

Drew caught John's eye, shook his head and with a flick of his eyes indicated that he should leave. "John doesn't want to be filmed and interviewed and I still want to know who your editor is, my friend," said Drew.

The young man continued to film John as he walked away, "I'm in a public place and I am free to film people. You can't censor me. He has blood on his hands," he shouted in a quivering voice.

"I've no intention of censoring you, but your media organisation must comply with editorial guidelines. You can see that John doesn't consent to being interviewed. May we have a civilised chat?" said Drew, in honeyed tones.

"You're not going to get away with this Mr de Witt!" the man shouted as he filmed John walking away. John simply continued and responded with an extended middle finger.

Drew winced as he saw John's rude gesture and repeated, "A civilised chat?"

"Okay, but I will keep the camera going," said the young man insistently.

"Whatever makes you happy. I'm Andrew," said Drew as he offered the young man his hand. They shook hands. Drew indicated a bench nearby and they both sat down.

"I assume you're his bodyguard or public relations goon," said the young man.

"You're wrong on both counts. I'm guiding John on the *Camino*. My name is Andrew and you are…" Drew paused, smiled and nodded. And paused. And smiled.

"Nick," the young man blurted out, to break the awful silence.

"Okay, Nick. May I say how impressed I am that you have staged this encounter. Must have taken a lot of technical skills, far more than I have," Drew laughed. "You deserve more than what you've got."

"What do you mean?" said Nick, suspecting some sort of trickery.

"Well, you've got a couple of questions fired at John. Some footage of him being agitated, saying the f-word and flicking you the finger. I think you deserve more than that. I presume from your accent you're a Brit and it must have taken some logistics to get here. Am I right in thinking you're a freelancer?"

"A 'social media influencer' I prefer to call

myself," said Nick.

"Fair enough. So this is what's going to happen. You're going to use the few seconds of video, plus a few minutes of scene setting and maybe even this conversation we're having. About right?"

"Yep. The public has a right to know," said Nick.

"Indeed they do. Oh yes, indeed they do. And now John will feel spooked by being buttonholed in the street, he'll give up on his pilgrimage, go home tonight and in no way feel the benefit The Way has to offer him. He'll probably be rightly pissed off I guess," explained Drew.

"Probably. Not my circus, not my monkeys," said the young man wondering where the conversation was going.

"Or..." said Drew.

"Or. What?" said Nick, confused.

"There may be a way both John and you can come out of this positively," said Drew.

"Oh that's right. You're going to pay me off!" said Nick, in an accusatory way.

Drew laughed again, "Nick, I haven't got tuppence to scratch my bum with. I send begging letters to church mice.

"No. How about I tell John that you're a decent guy and are not going to broadcast the fifteen seconds of fame you have captured and he can complete his *Camino* in peace. And, in recognition of the time and money you've spent, give you a proper one-to-one interview back in the UK?"

There was a short pause. Nick then said, "Well how do I know John will give me an interview?"

"That's just it. You don't. He has to trust you that you won't use your footage as he would definitely then have to quit the *Camino*. And you have to trust him.

"Either way I don't give a stuff, as tomorrow I will keep on walking regardless. Think about it Nick. You always have the footage you've taken already, for whatever it's worth. I'll write my email address down and if you want a proper exclusive interview with John, let me know soon. How about it, Scoop?"

"Actually, Andrew, it's not such a bad idea," said Nick, thoughtfully.

"Hope to hear from you shortly Nick. I must be off, I have a young man to placate," said Drew with a chuckle and he strolled off towards the *albergue* with his hands in his pockets.

◆ ◆ ◆

Back in the *albergue* John had just finished packing his rucksack, in the otherwise empty dormitory.

"You leaving so soon, John?" said Drew, as he flopped onto his bunk.

"*Ja*. Too damn right! I've just been compromised," said John, clearly flustered. "You need to implement the extraction plan, send up the Bat Sign or whatever you gotta do. Get me the *fok* out of here, man!"

"Yes. Can do that," said Drew slowly, as he calmly lay back and put his hands behind his head. "Or maybe have a cup of tea and a chat with Uncle Peter. It's getting towards that time for our sitrep at six o'clock."

"How can you be so relaxed?" said John, in a slightly panicky way.

"The way I see it, is that some enterprising social media jerk has been alerted to your whereabouts, probably by some software; he's *schlepped* across here to Spain to knobble you in the street and get an *exposé*. Woohoo! He's got nothing apart from you saying the f-word. And giving him the finger was real class," Drew grinned. "Big deal! I think we can work with him. We can deal with other paparazzi in the same way if we have to. The problem is that if Nick can find you, maybe some bad *hombres* can do so as well. They might want to stick more than a camera and fluffy microphone in your face."

"Who the hell is Nick?" demanded John.

"He's the very nice chap we just spoke to in the street," said Drew, as a ping notification alert came from his phone, "and he's the guy who has just sent me an email... Oh, he has agreed not to use the footage he has taken today."

"Oh and you believe him?" said John, sarcastically.

"Well he might, he might not. If we trust him, maybe you can give him a grown-up interview in the UK in the future.

"Right, it's a bit early for our regular catchup, but let's call Peter and give him the good news," said Drew, as he initiated a video call.

Peter looked surprised to see both Drew and John on the video call, "Alright what's happened?"

"We had a close encounter of the journalistic kind, Dixie," said Drew.

"Ah crap! Was it about the devil dog story or something to do with the photo of the ID card you emailed to me last night?" said Peter.

"Oh no. Nothing to do with the dog bite and that photo is something completely different. I will tell you about that guy later," said Drew, remembering the meeting with the muggers in Burgos.

"Okay, getting compromised by the press was always a possibility. Let's get you both out of there," said Peter, in a resigned way.

"Cool your jets Pete, before you make a knee-jerk decision. I'm not convinced it is as bad as all that. I will let Andrew fill you in," said John.

Drew explained to Peter what had happened in the street in Hornillos; the conversation with Nick, and his agreement to not go public, in anticipation of an exclusive interview at some point in the future. Peter took some convincing that carrying on the *Camino* was still viable.

"Okay, okay. I will get the extraction plan warmed up, just in case I need to pull the trigger and get you both out of there. In the meantime, our analysts will work doubly hard to see if any other wannabee journos want to try and win the Pulitzer Prize by getting John 'Pottymouth' de Witt to tell them to eff off. If you get any negative vibes, gut feelings, what I call 'bad atmospherics' just shout up and I will get you outta there pronto," said Peter.

"That's fine by me. By the way you will only need one seat in the rescue helicopter. I'm staying on *Camino*, even if my pal John here has to go home by chopper," said Drew.

"Alright. Apart from that. As always, any scandal, gossip, rumour or smut?" said Peter.

"Ah yes. Before I forget we were nearly robbed last night in Burgos," said Drew. "One of the two guys had that ID card on him, I sent you."

"Dunno why you wait till now to tell me about it," said Peter. "Never a dull moment with you two. So, what the bloody hell happened?"

Drew explained about the two attackers and how they were put out of action. He went on to say that they only spoke in Spanish to him so it was unlikely that they knew who they were. The muggers were probably just chancers.

"I agree with your hypothesis. Had a 'friend of a friend' check out that ID card. Diego is quite the local talent. Lots of previous convictions for assault, robbery and pickpocketing. Has a younger brother called Matias, who also has form for mugging tourists. Sounds like you taught them both a lesson they won't forget in a hurry.

"I will get my IT elves to see if anything is brewing in the land of Burgos *Policía Local* which could come up to bite us on the arse. Anything else you have forgotten to tell me?" said Peter.

"As always, no. Goodnight Dixie," said Drew, he disconnected the video call.

"How do you feel about going to mass and receiving a pilgrim blessing John?" asked Drew.

"I'm NGK," said John.

"What's that?"

"I'm Dutch Reformed Church," said John.

"That's fine. The church is Roman Catholic, but it doesn't matter. Just don't take the communion."

"Are you trying to convert me?" said John.

"Last thing I'd try to do. Apart from spirituality, it's an effective counter-surveillance opportunity. And if you get a blessing from Him upstairs it can't harm. We could always do with a bit more help on our side," said Drew.

◆ ◆ ◆

At 7 pm the priest started the mass. The congregation was half locals, mainly elderly women, as well as pilgrims. Drew looked around to see if there were any potential hostiles.

Drew could not understand most of what the priest said, but 'followed the crowd' in standing, sitting and kneeling at the appropriate times. After communion the mass ended and the priest invited the pilgrims to approach the altar where he distributed a printed sheet containing a pilgrim blessing in several languages.

When it came to the English version Drew and John read aloud the blessing.

As they left the church John said, "I was alright with the stuff about 'We humbly beseech your blessing' but when it got to the '...arrive safe and well at the end... [and] may they go home full of your love...'" he had to stop and take a breath. "I mean tears were flowing. What the *fok* is this walk doing to me man?"

"Obviously not curbing your profanities," Drew said laughing. "Time for dinner, John?"

Drew felt a small glow of satisfaction. His first proper security test on the *Camino*, and he thought he had not done too bad. Of course, Security Czar Dixie would see it in black and white and want to extract John, but Drew considered that a diplomatic solution had been arrived at. Of course everything still had the potential to go wrong and the soft and pungent could still hit the fan, but so far he was pleased with the result.

As for the attack in Burgos, the two would-be muggers would not be facing any charges, but would not be in a rush to cause Drew or John any problems for quite a while.

◆ ◆ ◆

The bar across the street from the church had a small restaurant area and the pair joined a friendly Australian couple on their table. Peter and Bronwyn, his wife, were heavily involved in refurbishing their sizeable beach house in New South Wales.

The conversation about fixing the house and Bronwyn's imminent return for a family wedding kept the talk away from John. As they had clam and white bean stew for starters, followed by pork in a mushroom sauce, Drew noticed that Peter appeared unhappy that he would soon be continuing on *Camino* alone; though not too unhappy.

Drew and John wished the Australian couple goodnight and they left to return to the *albergue*, conscious of the fact that it closed its doors at 10 pm, promptly.

15. HORNILLOS TO CASTROJERIZ

<u>464 km to Santiago de Compostela.</u>

At 6 am Drew checked his phone. As he expected there was an email from Dixie:

> 'Wakey! Wakey! Hands off snakey!
> The social media guy is probably Nicholas Bradley. I'm told he's a budding "content creator", whatever the hell that means. Checked all news feeds. No reporting of yesterday's meeting. Good work matey. Crack on.'

Drew and John walked through Hornillos del Camino in the dark. As it was still early they carried their trekking poles, rather than upset the locals with the tapping sound they made on the road.

Drew adjusted his scarf to keep out the cold and was glad he had put on his windcheater.

"Brr! Cold," was all John said.

As they left the street lit village the cloudless sky treated the pair to a dazzling array of stars. On the horizon there were dozens of red blinking lights from massive wind farms.

Drew said, "Breakfast partner, *bon appetito*!"

as he handed John a sachet of salt, 'liberated' some time previously from a popular fast food restaurant, and two boiled eggs.

"Well how about you filling me in on your connections with mercenaries?" asked Drew.

"'Private military contractors' actually. That must have come as a bit of a shock to you when that guy confronted me yesterday, eh?" said John, smiling to himself in the dark.

"More of a surprise rather than a shock. I checked out the De Witt business online and there was something which just didn't add up," said Drew, peeling the shell from an egg.

"How we had become so successful just distributing tractors and ploughs?" asked John.

"Yes, that's about the size of it. I thought there were 'other services' your company was offering," said Drew, double checking that all the shell was removed before sprinkling a little salt on the egg.

"I haven't been personally involved with it. Our Specialist Training and Consultancy Division is something which my dad has kept me well away from. He had served in South African special forces and on operations in Angola in the 1970s. I've just been exposed to the more 'agricultural' side of the business," said John, following Drew's lead and peeling an egg as they walked.

"You've got to anticipate this will change when you take the reins from Paul, eventually" said Drew, in between eating his boiled egg.

John accepted that the PMC business was

'shadowy' and there was a lack of transparency. The main De Witt business was selling or leasing agricultural plant and machinery, as well as offering training and maintenance. Behind the scenes De Witt also used their contacts, experience and expertise to assist countries which were friendly to South Africa, where necessary. This usually involved the training of government troops and pilots, plus some advisors in operational theatres. Obviously, the South African government and the third party countries insisted on utmost discretion.

There was some discussion about a failed African coup a few years ago. "Our company had nothing at all to do with that cluster *fok-up*," John said, emphatically. "It is a case study in how not to run a clandestine operation. Anyway the future is a professional setup. Countries embark on expeditionary operations for national security reasons, say in Iraq and Afghanistan, but the political reality is that they don't want their own 'boots on the ground' to be on the ground for a second longer than they have to. This is where our PMC can come in to help bridge the gap between the war-fighting element and the restoration of normality."

John explained his intention to Drew that, when he could, he would create a separate division of the business with 'clear blue water' between the plant and machinery arm and the PMC.

"I want transparency. Our military contractor

division is a professional and legitimate business," said John.

"Your 'customers' are not going to be happy with their contracts being used as a 'white paper case study' on your website."

"You're probably right, but there is lots of good work which we do, like training pilots for humanitarian missions. Or protecting workers at a water purification facility which we can highlight or supplying a military base with canteens and latrines which are not at all contentious. All good publicity," said John.

Drew felt reassured that John had plans for what he intended to do, come the day he took over from his father. Whether he could make the changes remained to be seen.

◆ ◆ ◆

As they were talking, Drew realised just how vulnerable they were. In the middle of nowhere in the pre-dawn. Anyone could creep up on them. He turned around and looked behind him. Nothing, though something caught Drew's attention as the beam from his head torch swung across a farmer's field. Something reflected the light back at him.

"John, take a look at this," said Drew, as he swung the light across the field. Again, the light reflected from an object. At first Drew thought it was a piece of reflective material from a discarded hi-visibility vest.

"*Fok*. It's a pair of eyes shining at us," said John, slightly concerned.

Drew could just make out two green-golden unblinking eyes. He guessed they were about 100 metres away, in the middle of the bare field.

"Being pedantic, they are 'reflecting' rather than 'shining' but you're right. Something is out there and it's looking at us," concluded Drew.

"Is it a person?" asked John.

"No. Our eyes reflect red. So I guess it's an animal. Probably not a cat, we're too far from habitation. Maybe a deer," ventured Drew.

"Or a wild boar? Or even a wolf?" suggested John.

"Hmm, let's hope not," said Drew, as they continued, at a slightly faster pace.

◆ ◆ ◆

After San Bol the men caught up with an Australian pilgrim called Linton, walking alone. They chatted, as pilgrims do, about The Way and the weather. From time to time they stopped to look behind them at the coming sunrise.

"Here, I will play you the *Camino* Song on my phone if I can get it to bloody work," said Linton. The sun rose and they all stood in awe. The Aussie played them the song by Dan Mullins about the *Camino* called 'Somewhere Along The Way.'

When the song finished John broke the silence, "Thanks mate. I will remember this moment."

The pair walked on.

◆ ◆ ◆

The next town the pilgrims came to was Hostanas, hidden in a dip in the otherwise flat expanse of farmland.

Outside of the first café they spotted The Young Crowd, who were occupying a couple of tables.

"Fancy a second breakfast?" asked Drew.

"*Ja. Lekker,*" John replied.

Drew greeted The Young Crowd, Pádraig, Siobhán, Sam, James and the others.

Inside the café, Drew took a table while John went to the counter and returned with their coffees and pastries. John was trying a *cortado* rather than his usual *café con leche*. Before they finished their drinks they had been joined by their Australian dinner partners from the previous evening, Peter and Bronwyn.

The two men cleared their table and set off again.

"It feels like a real community," observed John. "Everyone is so friendly."

"Glad you've found that. I hope that this companionable attitude travels back with everyone," said Drew. "Some say that the *Camino* only really starts when you get to Santiago."

They also bumped into Linton as they were

leaving the café.

After a few minutes John observed, "We were walking so much faster than Linton, but in the minutes we spent in the café he caught up with us."

"Often the case. You go hell for leather only for a slow coach to catch you up at a break. Makes you think about just going at a nice saunter. You'll get there, sooner or later."

◆ ◆ ◆

Eventually the men came to the massive archway which spanned the road to Castrojeriz, the Convento San Anton.

"Wow. I've seen this on videos of the *Camino.* It's even more impressive in reality," said John.

Drew agreed. They took a break and wandered around the ruins of the convent. If these walls could talk, thought Drew, what secrets would they tell?

It was no coincidence that the convent was built on the *Camino,* as the Antonianos order was devoted to tending to pilgrims. Drew reflected on the fact that he was following in the Antonianos' footsteps by looking after John and protecting him.

"Hi there. Glad I've caught up with you again," said Tom, the Chicago lawyer who they shared dinner with in Belorado.

"Oh hi," said John. Drew was within earshot,

but found something interesting on his phone.

"Meant to say that online the Burgos newspaper is interested in an interview with you for saving that guy's life after he was bitten. Let me get the appeal they put out on social media," Tom started to check his phone. Drew wondered how John would deal with this.

"It's okay man," said John, "I need to put you in the picture." Drew cringed as he assumed that John would disclose his status, he need not have worried.

"To tell you the truth, I'm actually meant to be on sick leave from work. I've got an internship with a Spanish company and they'd go nuts if they picked on the fact that I was on *Camino*. Can we keep this just between ourselves Tom?" John said, conspiratorially.

"Oh okay. I didn't realise. It makes sense now how you tried to deflect the conversation at dinner the other night. See you around, partner," said Tom.

Drew put on his rucksack and walked on with John.

"Nicely done," said Drew.

Soon Castrojeriz came into view, with an ancient castle on the hill above the town.

16. CASTROJERIZ

It seemed like Castrojeriz had been evacuated. The pair walked through its deserted streets. The occasional vehicle passing through gave hope that they had not suffered an apocalypse.

It was often the case in Spain that there was a flurry of activity in the mornings, followed by a lull, before the villages came back to life in the evenings. This was the rhythm of life in Castrojeriz.

As they arrived in town early, the two men had the pick of the lodgings. John looked hopefully at some of the boutique deluxe hotels and fancy *casa rurals*, but Drew was looking for something else. At Casa Nostra he found the ideal billet. An old care-worn *albergue* which offered little in the way of creature comforts apart from showers, toilets, beds, WiFi and a basic kitchen.

"In a previous life Drew, were you a monk?" asked John, as he sorted his kit out on the top bunk and looked despairingly around the spartan room.

"Hey, it's not the Ritz, but it allows us to merge with the herd," said Drew, "and all for ten *euros* a night."

A *peregrina* joined the dormitory, a Japanese woman called Lena who they had met on The

Way. Although fifty, she looked much younger and exuded a positive spirit and a flashed great smile.

As the pair were going through their afternoon routine, they were joined by two Frenchmen they had seen previously. They had also attended mass at Hornillos del Camino the night before. They were friendly, but their inability to speak English, as well as Drew's inability to speak French, hampered communication.

Drew put his head torch on to charge it up.

"Don't you find it strange that all morning we exercise like crazy, walking twenty to thirty kilometres, then we arrive somewhere in the afternoon and simply *sit gat, rus bene*?" asked John. Using the delightful *Afrikaaner* expression to, sit on your arse and rest your legs.

"Fair comment," said Drew. "I think of it as an alternative to a rest day. Many pilgrims take a rest day, or a 'zero kilometre day' every week or so, but if I take an afternoon rest it has the same recuperative effect."

"Or so you reckon," John said, sceptically.

Two more pilgrims were set to join the dormitory before the night was done. The first was a young Polish woman, who was a teacher of English based in Bilbao. She was very insistent on leaving the dormitory window wide open. Drew was not going to argue, but thought she would quickly change her mind later if it got cold or noisy, or both. She did not offer her name, but went through a series of stretching and yoga exercises whilst Drew averted his gaze, mostly.

There was still one last bed to fill before the dormitory was *completo*.

◆ ◆ ◆

As usual at 6 pm Drew started a video call and Peter answered it, "Hola Dixie."

"Hola Drew. Whatcha. Anything to report today?"

"Nope. All quiet on the *Camino* front."

Peter cringed, "Oh I wish you wouldn't use the Q-word. It is the harbinger of doom in the security world. We've got a problem, matey."

"What?" said Drew.

"Not what. Who," said Peter.

"Okay. Who?" asked Drew.

"Amanda," said Peter.

"Who is Amanda?" asked Drew.

"Dunno," said Peter.

"Must say you're not making much sense today, Dixie. Should I just hang up and try again?"

"It's a stalker called Amanda. We haven't heard anything from her for over a year now, but our IT backroom boys have discovered she's flown from South Africa to Europe, and now she's in Madrid. She made the move just after John's whereabouts flashed up from the photo taken at Santo Domingo. Got to conclude she's coming for him," said Peter, his eyes were looking baggy and dark, as if he had been up all night.

"Well I'm sure if Amanda turns up with a rose behind her ear, John and I can deal with her," said Drew, confidently.

"Oh you don't know how dangerous she is matey," Peter said gravely. "I will give you the intelligence briefing on her. It has been updated today. Will email it to you for 'your eyes only.' Call me back when you've read it," Peter disconnected from the meeting.

Drew's phone pinged a few seconds later. He had an email from Peter with an attachment named 'Amanda'. Drew opened the document and read it with increasing concern.

In summary, an unknown person calling herself Amanda believed that she was in a romantic relationship with John de Witt. This started after a photograph of John appeared in a South African fashion magazine showing him at a charity ball with his arm around the slim waist of a supermodel.

Amanda's emails were full of delusional nonsense and she had requested an urgent face-to-face meeting with John. When no response was forthcoming, Amanda passed bogus material to the media. Her emails became increasingly aggressive and very disturbing. The derogatory term for a predatory woman, 'man-eater', was all too accurate if what Amanda was planning to do to John, in her sickeningly explicit emails, came true.

Drew recontacted Peter on a video call.

"Have you read the report?" said Peter.

"Unfortunately, yes. I'm not a psychologist, but Amanda has some demons in her head," Drew said soberly, feeling nauseous thinking about what she proposed to do to John, once she had drugged him.

Peter said, "I usually have the 'pleasure' of assessing the risks posed by all the odd-balls who try to contact John or his dad, including the female cranks. I have a database aptly named, 'Gold diggers, sperm stealers, bunny boilers and control freaks.' This Amanda has the motivation to cause real harm to John. She is off the scale dangerous."

"It looks like she might get the opportunity to get to him if she has travelled all the way to Spain," said Drew.

"All she needs is to get him isolated, give him a paralytic sedative and carry out her fantasy plan. Have you read what she intends to do?" asked Peter.

"Yes. I kind of wish I hadn't. Extreme violence, with an unhealthy dose of kinky cannibalistic fetish?"

"That just about covers it," said Peter. "We use a guy here from the South African police high-tech crime unit. He deduced that Amanda saw an image of John on a *Camino* forum social media site. She knows he's on the *Camino* and she's heading your way matey."

"What's on your mind?" asked Drew.

"Truthfully, I'm a hair's breadth from

exfiltrating John," said Peter. He sounded exhausted as if he had been wrestling with the various options of dealing with Amanda.

"Okay. I think that's the safest option. How about I brief John, full disclosure. And see what he says," said Drew.

"Agreed. Tell him my recommendation is to extract him, but it is up to him," said Peter.

◆ ◆ ◆

Drew found John lying on his bunk, "John we need to have a discreet chat."

They went into the empty kitchen in the *albergue* and Drew explained the threat assessment posed by Amanda; Peter's recommendation to leave the *Camino*, and asked for his thoughts.

John paused to reflect on what Drew had told him. "What do you think I should do?" he asked.

"Whoa, John. I've got no 'skin in the game' here. I'm not the target and I'm not employed by Peter. It has to be your decision," said Drew.

"Okay. I won't hold you to it, but if you were me. What would you do?"

"You put me in a difficult position," said Drew, "but I think I would continue on the *Camino*, increase my vigilance, and if Peter gets any more intelligence on Amanda's whereabouts, reassess. But it has gotta be your call."

After a while John said, "I'm really benefiting

from being on the *Camino* with you. It's doing me far more good than any clinic could do. I'd hate to pull out right now. So I will stay and see what happens."

"Oh God. I'll be sleeping with one eye open from now on," said Drew, with a nervous laugh.

"Me too," said John.

◆ ◆ ◆

Drew reconnected with Peter on a video call for the third time and explained the plan.

"Alright. I don't like it. I don't like it one little bit, but we'll go with it. Keep your phone handy matey, and switched on at all times, in case I need to call you in a hurry," said Peter.

"Will do."

"Wish I could give you more information about Amanda so you know who to look out for. I don't know what she looks like or even if she's a South African, her digital footprint simply locates her here. Have you seen any odd women?" asked Peter.

Drew immediately thought of Ellen, but excluded her as she had made contact with John before Amanda set off from South Africa. Then he thought about the Japanese and the Polish women who they are sharing the dormitory with. Or, maybe one of The Young Crowd. But hell, half the pilgrims were female.

"No. I will keep an eye out though," said Drew.

"By the way, I've got an update on your two Burgos buddies," said Peter.

"Oh Alfonso and his wife? How are they doing?" asked Drew, assuming Peter meant the couple who were attacked by the Doberman.

"No, the 'other' buddies, Diego and Matias. You know your 'tears before bedtime' in the side street buddies," said Peter.

"Oh yes. I almost forgot them. How are the lads?" Drew asked, as if they were long-lost nephews.

"The *Policía Local* responded to the intruder alarm, according to their dispatch database," said Peter. "They arrested the two brothers. There was insufficient evidence, and no CCTV footage, so they were released the following day. The boys accounted for their injuries by saying that they had a bust-up with each other. A 'family matter' they said. Allegedly, one of them had besmirched the reputation of their mother. Neither wanted to press charges against the other."

"Ah. That's nice of them," Drew wanted to know how Peter had access to the police database and, at the same time, he did not want to know. He doubted that even Peter would have the technical resources to hack a secure police computer system. It was far more likely that he had someone in the law enforcement community who was feeding him insider information.

"All's well, that ends well. Goodnight Dixie. John and I don't want to be late for mass," said

Drew and disconnected.

♦ ♦ ♦

The pair continued with their masquerade of piety and attended the 7 pm mass at Iglesia de San Juan, with a pilgrim blessing after.

During the service John whispered to Drew, "You don't understand the Spanish mass, do you?"

"Not really, but if there is a God it doesn't matter. The fact is we have turned up. If He is all knowing then He will be aware."

Drew scanned the congregation, taking an intense professional interest in female pilgrims, searching for Amanda.

After mass the pair stopped at the Bar Plaza. Casual observers may have noticed that the two men at an outside table having burgers were looking a little too intently at single females walking past.

Tom strolled past and put his index finger to his lips and winked at John.

♦ ♦ ♦

When the men returned to their *albergue* they met the last to join their dormitory. The pilgrim greeted both of them with a firm handshake, "Hi there. I'm Davie, Davie Anderson," in a broad Scottish accent.

Davie had the typical Scots fair complexion and ginger hair with a beard. Drew reckoned he was in his mid-30s and had the physique of a Rugby front row forward.

It was an exhausting day for Drew and John, who quickly got into their bunks.

It had obviously also been a tiring day for Davie. He spent a lot of time sorting out his stuff and fussing about with the charging of his phone.

◆ ◆ ◆

In Cleveland Ohio at the School of Film and Media Arts CSU a student ran the Belfast 1983 video tape on an old VHS player he had managed to get working. Once he had adjusted the tracking, the footage was of surprisingly good quality.

Some sort of military patrol had walked into an ambush in an urban area.

The infantry grunt on point had been taken out by an explosion. There was gunfire and as the smoke was clearing the squad leader looked paralysed. A uniformed woman was seen to be engaging with the leader before she ran to drag the downed point guy into cover. The student gasped as the woman was shot and fell onto the leader of the squad.

He converted the VHS analogue image to digital, added metadata and uploaded the content to the internet.

A chain reaction had started.

17. CASTROJERIZ TO FRÓMISTA

444 km to Santiago de Compostela.

Drew and John set off very early from Castrojeriz. The threat posed by Amanda had made them both uneasy, neither had slept soundly. They crept out of the dormitory so as not to disturb the others.

The Way from Castrojeriz would lead them into the *Meseta* proper, the tableland of flat arable land, with a steep 100 metre ascent.

Before they got to the incline the pair walked quietly through the sleepy town. A massive illuminated yellow arrow was projected onto the side of Iglesia San Juan, indicating the route. The first half hour was spent walking through dark farmland. The moonlight was insufficient to walk safely, so Drew used his head torch.

Up ahead the pair could see torch light, part way up the hill. Another pilgrim was slogging their way up the incline. Soon enough, the two men started up the steep rocky path and got into their hill climbing routine. They shortened their step and adjusted their breathing - when bad luck struck.

"Sod it!" said Drew, as his head torch died.

"Thought you'd charged it up last night," said John, in the pitch dark.

"So did I," said Drew. "Damn it. Will have to use the torch on my phone."

Just then they saw a head torch of a pilgrim coming up the hill from Castrojeriz and in a couple of minutes their new friend Davie joined them.

"*Och*, it's you two *roaming* in the *gloaming*," said the friendly Scotsman.

Drew explained that his head torch had failed. Davie offered to walk with them until dawn.

"You're our guardian angel man!" announced John.

"*Och aye*. As they say 'The *Camino* Provides,'" replied Davie, cheerfully.

Drew recalled that someone told him that on *Camino*, pilgrims experience about five per cent more luck than they would have otherwise got. Such as the chance that, just when his own head torch failed in the dark, another pilgrim would miraculously appear to help them out.

With Drew preoccupied with keeping vigilant for Amanda, having Davie as an ally could well be an advantage. Drew was also annoyed with himself. He was certain he had fully charged his head torch and could not understand why it had failed on him.

"Two is one: One is none," Drew muttered to himself.

"What does that mean?" asked John.

"I feel so stupid to rely on just one light. If I had two, when my one torch packed up I would still have another one."

"Don't want to say I told you so," said John.

"*Och* well. Thank heavens I'm here," said Davie.

They reached the top of the hill and after a steep slope downwards were onto the *Meseta*. As the sun rose, the farmland stretched ahead, and all around, to the horizon.

The three men walked on in a loose formation. Drew was happy to take up a position at the back. He could 'vet' any lone *peregrina* if they approached. By engaging them in a 'field interview' disguised as polite conversation, he hoped to confirm if they were Amanda the South African psychopath or not.

He could see that John and Davie were getting on well, chatting from time to time. Davie could be a very useful 'extra pair of hands' if an Amanda-shaped crisis occurred, Drew thought.

◆ ◆ ◆

Eventually on the left side of the road they came to an isolated building like a chapel. It was the Antigua Ermita de San Nicolás. It was famous as an old hospital for pilgrims. It did not have mod-cons such as electricity, so the lucky pilgrims who stayed overnight were treated to an authentic taste of mediaeval times.

They crossed the bridge and marched into the village of Itera de la Vega, where they took a break.

"For a place which has 'La Vega' in its name I was expecting more," said John, as he looked despondently around the quiet village.

"Some entertainment perhaps?" offered Davie, with a wink.

"Yes. I wasn't expecting *Cirque du Soleil*, but-" said John.

"*Och aye*, but a few wee dancing girls maybe?" said Davie, jokingly.

Drew was amused by Davie's broad Glaswegian accent. It sounded like he had been binge-watching Scottish standup comedians.

"A coffee and *croissant* would be *lekker*," said John, as he stared at his water bottle and munched on a cereal bar. Drew and Davie dug deep into their rucksacks and managed to amass a poor man's lunch of three apples and a few plastic wrapped muffins.

Drew was happy that, without prompting, John took the chance to check his blisters and swap his socks for fresh ones. After a few minutes the three men put on their rucksacks and set off.

"Let's get out of this shithole," said Davie, unequivocally.

◆ ◆ ◆

The path was straight and the landscape flat. They passed through Boadilla del Camino without stopping, as Drew reckoned they were not far from the end of their day's walk, Frómista.

The Way led onto the towpath of the Canal de Castille for the last few kilometres of the day. The pilgrims crossed the footbridge over the canal.

They followed the signs to the municipal *albergue* which they found on the Plaza San Martin just before it opened at 1.30 pm.

◆ ◆ ◆

Computer algorithms at Lagan Live News Today in Belfast automatically detected the metadata about an incident during The Troubles in Belfast. It brought the video to the news editor's computer screen.

Paul Byrne was on a video call with his Political Correspondent, Harry Curtis, when the notification of a new video popped up, "Yeah, Harry I hear you pal, but the machinations of the Stormont Assembly are as dull as ditchwater."

"But you have to understand Paul that what's being proposed will affect all the primary schools in the Province. I'll start at the beginning so I will..." said Harry.

Paul stifled a yawn and clicked on the play icon of the incoming video clip.

As Harry droned on, the video of the bombing and gun attack in Belfast from 1983 unfolded. "Holy Mother of God!" shouted Paul.

"What?" said a very puzzled Harry.

"Sorry, Harry. Something's just cropped up. I'll have to ring you back," and ended the video call.

"Róisín!" bellowed Paul.

Róisín Sullivan, a veteran investigative journalist, came into Paul's office.

"What's up now, Paul?" asked Róisín, the coolest head in any crisis a newsroom could have.

"A ghost from the past," said Paul and briefed Róisín on the shocking video he had just witnessed, from a time before she was born.

A few hours later, Róisín identified where and when the incident was filmed and linked it to several contemporary news reports.

It was child's play for her to search the internet for Corporal Peter Dickinson B.E.M. and find that he now worked for De Witt's as their Director of Security.

18. FRÓMISTA

The three men booked into the *albergue* and shared a large dormitory room with several other male pilgrims.

At least Amanda would stand out a mile if she turned up in here, Drew concluded. He plugged in his troublesome head torch to charge it up. Drew reflected on how well he and John were prepared in case Amanda made a move against them, especially with their new *amigo*, Davie Anderson, on their side.

Drew left John and Davie in the *albergue* whilst he went to the *supermercado* to buy snacks and fruit for the following day. When he got back to the dormitory, he saw that his head torch was still charging up. Somehow it had practically gone flat overnight in Castrojeriz. Bloody technology, thought Drew and hoped it would not let him down again.

The three pilgrims had finished showering and sorting out their kit. They indulged in a couple of hours of light napping.

◆ ◆ ◆

At just after 6 pm Drew was in the walled garden of the *albergue* when he started his video call with, "*Hola* Dixie, how's it hanging?"

"Alright. How's your day?" asked Peter.

"Uneventful. Apart from my damn head torch packing up half way up the hill out of Castrojeriz. Luckily Davie was not far behind and helped us to see where we were going," said Drew.

"Who's Davie?" asked Peter.

"A Scotsman we met up with last night, called Davie Anderson. He cracks me up, sounds like Billy Connolly. Anyway, any news from Amanda?" asked Drew, apprehensively.

"Nothing heard. She has gone suspiciously quiet, matey. My IT elves are baffled. They are still convinced she is in Spain though," said Peter.

"How do they figure that?" asked Drew, almost hoping that Amanda was imaginary.

"Because it doesn't appear she has left. If she moved out of Spain, I reckon my IT guys would have known," said Peter.

"Seems a bit weird. Anyway, tonight we are in an all-male dorm so we should be okay. We are heading off for an evening of organ recital and Gregorian chanting at the church. After that we'll find dinner somewhere."

"Enjoy. If I hear anything I will contact you direct, so keep your phone on, matey," said Peter.

◆ ◆ ◆

At 7 pm, Drew and John went to Iglesia de San Pedro for a cultural experience of organ music and a male soloist singing Gregorian chants.

Looking around the congregation in the magnificent old church were the 'usual suspects,' the two French guys, some of The Young Crowd, Carlos, a Spanish pilgrim and a few others Drew knew by sight.

He scanned the faces, particularly any new lone females who could be Amanda. Reassuringly, he saw no *femme fatales* in the congregation. Or so he hoped.

Drew was able to close his eyes and let the organ music wash over him. For a few minutes he forgot he was minding John and protecting him from Amanda, the psychopathic stalker.

◆ ◆ ◆

At the end of the performance the pair filed out of the church and they met Davie waiting outside.

"Have you eaten?" asked Drew.

"Nah. I'm starving. My belly thinks my throat's been cut," laughed Davie.

Drew spotted Carlos and three other pilgrims walking across the road to a small restaurant.

"I guess Carlos will lead us to a decent local place," said Drew.

The waiter at El Chiringuito del Camino seated Drew, John and Davie at the last available table. The place was packed. Most of the customers were locals and the room was filled with loud conversation.

The menu was limited, but the specialities of the house were racks of ribs or *Burgos morcilla*, the blood pudding with rice. The three men had voracious appetites and ate like wolves.

"Did you hear the big news today?" asked Davie.

"No. What's happened?" asked John.

"A Spaniard was reported as saying, 'Well that's all I have to say on this subject,'" said Davie, laughing.

John looked bemused.

"Do you not *ken* it? The bloody Spaniards just *canna* stop talking. They're probably born *blethering* on," said Davie.

Drew and John agreed that the culture in Spain is to talk, loud and often.

John spoke to Carlos who was on the next table and thanked him for showing them the way to the fabulous restaurant, but when John turned back to face Drew and Davie he looked decidedly unhappy.

"You have a face like a bulldog licking piss off a nettle. What's up *laddie*?" asked Davie.

"Carlos says that Carrión is full. Everything has been booked up. Accommodation is impossible," said John, looking crestfallen.

"Damn it," said Drew. He knew this was going to happen one day. They had ridden their luck. There were at least a hundred pilgrims in Frómista that night and a growing anxiety about beds. This had resulted in a spate of pilgrims booking ahead.

"Do you know what impossible means?" asked Davie, seemingly unfazed by the announcement that Carrión de los Condes was full.

"What?" asked John, slightly depressed.

"Do you *ken* word games? 'Impossible' actually means 'I'm possible.' And, as luck would have it, I booked myself an AirBnB in Carrión for tomorrow night, when you two were in the *kirk*," said Davie, with a smug look.

"And how does that help us?" asked John.

"The *bonnie wee* AirBnB *hoose* has two twin bedrooms. You're welcome to join me. *Me casa tu casa*, as they bloody well say here," announced Davie.

Drew and John were delighted at their good fortune and insisted on paying for Davie's dinner.

"Well. This means a lie-in tomorrow!" said John, beaming.

❖ ❖ ❖

Back in the dormitory Drew did not bother setting an alarm. At least tomorrow morning I won't have to rely on my head torch, thought Drew as he settled down to sleep.

Drew overheard Davie chatting with Linton, the slow Australian pilgrim, in the bunk above him. Linton was lecturing Davie on *Camino* history in a most patronising manner.

"I must say *mon*," said Davie to his Aussie bunkmate in a positive tone, "You remind me of a *lighthoose* in the desert."

"Really?" said Linton, thinking he was being paid a compliment by his new found Scottish friend, "In what way mate?"

"Well for a start you're really very bright," said Davie.

"Ah. Thanks mate."

"And you certainly stand *oot*. And..."

"Yes. And..." prompted Linton

"You're totally bloody useless!" said Davie, laughing.

"Ah, *rack off you dag.*"

Drew grinned in the darkness as he heard Linton mutter, "Bloody Jock."

19. FRÓMISTA TO CARRIÓN

<u>419 km to Santiago de Compostela.</u>

By 8 am the three pilgrims, Drew, John and Davie, were sitting outside Café-bar Puzzles in Frómista taking, for once, a leisurely breakfast. Thanks to Davie, their new bestie, their beds in Carrión de los Condes that night were sorted.

They treated themselves to a second round of coffees, there would be no rush today. No stumbling around on The Way in the dark relying on a dodgy head torch. It still puzzled Drew how his own, up till then, reliable head torch had packed up on him on the previous morning.

The three discussed the route for the day. It would be less than 20 km, or four to five hours of walking, to get to Carrión mainly alongside the P-980. A few villages along The Way would break up the monotony and maybe provide a stress-free midday rest break.

Drew went into the bar to use the toilet, leaving John checking his phone and Davie packing his rucksack. When he came back out Davie also went into the bar to, in his own words, 'syphon the python.'

"Think I'm neurotic, but I sometimes notice little things," said Drew.

"Okay Boss. What is it this time?" said John, assuming Drew had found yet another thing which irritated him.

"Oh it's nothing about you, this time. Whenever I put my water bottle back in the side pouch of my pack, the bottle's wrist strap always hangs out, but it's now tucked in. Weird. I never do that," said Drew.

"Oh I think Davie had to move your pack to get to his. He might have done it I suppose," said John.

"Ah! That explains things. It would have been bugging me otherwise," Drew said, with a chuckle.

When Davie rejoined them, they put on their rucksacks and Drew said, "Let's walk."

◆ ◆ ◆

Miss Else Badenhorst, the Communications Director for De Witt's, was hoping for a quiet day in the office when her PA called.

"Morning Else. Sorry to drop this on you, but I have had a call from a journalist in Northern Ireland, a Ms Sullivan or O'Sullivan I'm not quite sure which. She has information which she thinks will interest us."

"I bloody doubt that," said Else, tersely.

"Oh that's where you're wrong. You are going to need to hear what she has to say."

◆ ◆ ◆

Shortly after Drew, John and Davie left Café-bar Puzzles in Frómista, a Seat Ibiza parked up nearby.

The driver went in to the bar to order two espresso coffees, the woman sat outside checking her phone. She smiled with satisfaction as she watched a red flashing icon moving steadily North-West along the P-980.

◆ ◆ ◆

Drew adopted his usual position behind John and Davie as they made their way along the track parallel with the main road. Today was a good day, thought Drew. The previous night's meal was excellent, they slept well, had a decent breakfast, the route was easy and their accommodation was booked.

Within an hour they reached the first village, Población de Campos.

"Good place for a stop I think," suggested Drew.

"*Och*, we've only just started *mon*," said Davie, impatiently.

"What's up with you *Ouballie*? You normally want to bash on. Are we going too fast for you?" taunted John.

"I'm just feeling a bit under the weather this morning," said Drew. He had started to feel a bit light-headed.

"Was it the *morcilla* you had last night?" said John.

"Maybe that black puddin' was *bowfin*, you should have had the ribs like us. They were *blaster*, but *hoora* salty," said Davie, chugging noisily on his water bottle.

After a short break Drew got up a little unsteadily and said, "Okay, er, let's walk."

"Revenga de Campos is about half an hour away. We can stop there for a break if you need to. I'd get some water on board if I were you," suggested Davie, helpfully.

Drew stifled a yawn, shook his head and walked on, following the other two.

Get an 'effin grip! Drew thought. He tried to walk faster to keep up the pace. Come on soldier, dig those heels in, his inner Sergeant-Major ordered. It worked, briefly.

◆ ◆ ◆

Eventually Revenga came into view, which spurred Drew on. He could not seem to shake off the sleepiness he felt. It was as if he was walking through a cotton wool cloud. Having a lie-in had not done him any good at all.

John and Davie were sitting on the bench by the water fountain, waiting for Drew.

"How are you doing?" asked Davie.

"Oh I'm fine. I'm getting there," said Drew. "Remember Linton, that Aussie we met a few days ago John? He was slow, but he got there in the end."

He went to top up his water bottle at the

fountain, but Davie saved him.

"Don't use that. I think it's contaminated. I just tried it. It tastes like shite," said Davie.

The men had covered a third of the day's distance, but would need to keep going if Davie was to keep his appointment with the AirBnB hostess in Carrión, to get the key to their accommodation. They decided to push on.

On the track Drew just stared at John and Davie and tried his best to keep in contact with them. He definitely felt unwell - sleepy and nauseous. Walking was a struggle, almost like treading through treacle.

♦ ♦ ♦

After what seemed like an eternity, they arrived at Villalcázar de Sirga, about an hour's walk from Carrión.

Drew flopped onto a bench.

"You look like you could sleep for a week, *mon*," Davie observed.

"At least," Drew said, with a smile.

"If it's alright with you, I'm just going to push on to Carrión. I don't want to miss picking up the keys. I will see you later. Okay?" said Davie.

"But I don't know where the AirBnB place is Davie," said Drew, sleepily.

"It's alright John will come with me and he will message you. We'll get settled in, put the kettle on and see you in a *wee* bit when you get to Carrión.

It's no far. No rush," said Davie.

"Thanks Davie," said Drew. "You're a lifesaver."

John and Davie put their rucksacks on and walked on.

◆ ◆ ◆

Drew's eyelids closed and he dozed off for a few minutes, until woken by his phone ringing incessantly.

"Hi Dixie. Whassup?" said Drew, drowsily.

"Sorry. Did I wake you?" asked Peter.

"Nah. I've been having one of those mornings," Drew yawned. "Maybe it's old age setting in. Have you got an update on Amanda?"

"Might be a load of crap, but my IT folks say she's popped up on the dark web again," said Peter.

"Oh yeah," Drew drawled. "What's she said this time?"

"No way of knowing if this is true but I will read you the message she posted for her followers 'Made contact with John de Witt. I'm so close I can touch him. I can smell his scent. Soon I will look into his eyes and see the fear.' Then there's the usual crap about 'Slicing his liver' and 'Showing him his heart while it still beats.' As I say, it's all probably still the ramblings of a deluded mind," said Peter.

"Sounds like a work of fantasy," Drew suggested.

"Yeah. You're probably right. While I've got

you on the phone, how about an update?" asked Peter.

"All good. We're nearly in Carrión. The place is said to be chocker-block full tonight. John is just ahead. Davie is collecting the keys to our accommodation. I'm not far behind and haven't seen any strange new women who could be Amanda," said Drew.

"Okay. I'm a bit confused. Are you still actually with John?" asked Peter.

"Not actually Dixie. He's actually gone ahead with Davie to Carrión actually," said Drew.

Peter paused, "You've let John out of your sight? Damn it Drew. I'll terminate the call and I urge you to get a shagging move on and get back into contact with him."

"Alright. Don't worry. Will do," said Drew, slowly.

"Now!" shouted Peter.

"Okay, alright already," replied Drew.

Drew ponderously put the rucksack straps on his shoulders while he sat on the bench. He grabbed his water bottle to take another drink, his eyelids felt like lead.

◆ ◆ ◆

Drew woke up as his mobile phone rang. It was Dixie, again.

"Yep. I'm on my way Dixie. I am on my bloody way," said Drew, fighting the urge to curl up on the bench for a nap.

"Work of fantasy my arse!" exclaimed Peter, on the brink of panic. "I've just had a second message from Amanda on the dark web. I'm sending it to you now so you can read it." Drew's phone pinged as a new email was received:

> John has a chaperone.
> A fat old nonce called Andrew.
> Looks like he could do with a good long sleep.
> A MAN DA

Drew read it twice. He was shocked. Amanda was real and indeed close by.

"Have you read it?" said Peter, with a note of anxiety in his voice.

"Yes. I'm stunned. Not seen any suspicious women who could be Amanda," said Drew defensively.

"Matey, you sound drugged. What have you had today?" demanded Peter.

"The usual strong coffee, that's not going to make me drowsy," said Drew. Something in his memory was causing him concern. Something to do with the wrist strap of his water bottle being tucked into the pouch of his rucksack back in Frómista. John saying that Davie had moved his pack. Something about Davie talking about salty food all of the time and encouraging him to drink more water. He looked at his water bottle, "Dixie. I think my water's been spiked."

"Well we can only hope that John and Davie

can deal with Amanda if she confronts them. Can you get a lift to Carrión?" asked Peter.

"I mean I could try and flag someone down, but I'm staggering about like a drunk. I wouldn't give me a lift. I will empty this bottle and drink loads of fresh water from a fountain to flush out the Mickey Finn and make best speed to Carrión," said Drew as he re-read the email with Amanda's last message.

"Yeah matey, do your best. I will do what I can from here," said Peter, hurriedly.

"Before you go Dixie. How does Amanda sign off on her messages?" asked Drew.

"Just in capitals. You know AMANDA," said Peter.

"This last one you just sent me is odd. There's a space after the first A and before the D," said Drew, suddenly realising something awful.

"Yeah. What of it?" asked Peter.

"Oh crap! It's A MAN with the initials DA. It's Anderson! His name is Davie Anderson," announced Drew. "Amanda is not a female at all. He's played you like a fool Dixie. I've been keeping a lookout for a woman, but it was a man all along."

Dixie sighed as he understood finally that he had been duped, "Go! Go! Bloody go! For God's sake help John."

Drew hung up, shook his head, emptied the water from his bottle, drank copiously from the public water fountain, before setting off as fast as he could towards Carrión.

◆ ◆ ◆

In Frómista Isabella said, "Get us to Carrión de los Condes. Finally, it's showtime Juan." They left their table and scrambled to their car.

Juan jumped into the Seat Ibiza and tore off at speed, while Isabella tried frantically to fasten her seatbelt.

The car took the roundabout above the A-67 motorway virtually on two wheels.

"Get us to Carrión in one piece, *estúpido*!" shouted Isabella to Juan. "I have important calls to make."

◆ ◆ ◆

Only about an hour to go to Carrión, thought Drew, as he marched quickly along. Keep walking to wear off the sedative. Keep swigging water to purge the system. How did I miss the signs?

The faulty head torch was odd. It was as if someone had deliberately drained the battery in Castrojeriz, so it would fail on the following morning in the dark. Who benefits? Drew asked himself. It gave Davie the opportunity to help them and become their Knight in Shining Armour, their saviour.

He pushed on, but kept analysing what had happened. Davie had just appeared in Castrojeriz 'out of the blue.' He never mentioned where he had begun the *Camino Frances*. Most pilgrims would say that their starting point was Saint-Jean, Pamplona or Burgos. Not Davie. That should have raised Drew's suspicions.

Drew kept going, his mind still racing. His Scottish accent was wrong. Like someone trying a little too much to be a Glaswegian hard man.

He forced the pace and imagined visions of calamity happening to John at Davie's hands. Drew was worried about what was happening in Carrión. It was out of his control. He hoped that John was sufficiently security conscious and took steps to protect himself. He did not know what help Dixie could offer all the way from Johannesburg, probably nothing.

Drew's mind conjured up a nightmare situation where John had been given a paralytic drug, but could still feel every agonising sensation as Davie butchered him.

The kilometre markers were counting down the distance to Carrión de los Condes for Drew. He had breezed past several pilgrims who had greeted him with a, *'Buen Camino,'* which he scarcely acknowledged. They assumed he was in a race for the last bed in town.

He had passed the 2 km marker. Carrión was in his sights. What would he find when he got there? He dreaded thinking about it.

Bloody hope this is good news, thought Drew, as he answered his phone.

"Drew it's Dixie. Are you there yet matey?" asked Peter, hopefully.

"Not far. About a mile to go. Any update?" asked Drew, as calmly as he could whilst still forcing the pace.

"Not yet. Just rang to say you're right, Amanda is a pseudonym. The IT team has confirmed that the stalker is David Anderson. Even that is likely to be a false name," he paused.

"I have a feeling you've had another message," said Drew.

"Sorry Drew. Yes. 'Amanda', or should I say Davie, has just posted that he is with John and has boasted about what he is about to do to him," said Peter, in a matter of fact way. "You make your way as best you can towards Carrión. I will try and figure something out. Bye matey."

Drew tried to spur himself to get to Carrión in time to save John. He imagined himself to be a warrior monk, a Knights Templar, a soldier of God and protector of pilgrims. His pace quickened.

Nothing now would get in his way of trying to save the life of John de Witt.

20. CARRIÓN DE LOS CONDES

Although Drew had made good progress, it would not change the outcome for John.

The effects of the sedative were wearing off, but left him in an agitated state. He was determined to make amends and take positive action to get to John, at all costs.

A car from the direction of Carrión slowed down as it passed Drew. It turned off behind him, before braking sharply on the gravel. The doors were flung open and he heard at least one person running towards him. His gut feeling was that whoever they were, they were 'hostiles.'

Drew did not react. He did not turn around. He cast a long shadow along the trail in front of him and he saw the shadow of a figure closing in fast behind. Drew heard a man shout, "*Señor!*" He spun around to face the threat and saw a powerfully built man running at him. Definitely a hostile.

The man grabbed Drew's rucksack shoulder strap, shouting, "*Señor!*" Instinctively Drew raised his hands, grabbed the man's jacket and headbutted him on the bridge of the nose with a sickening crunch. The man bellowed and his momentum threw Drew onto his back.

Still holding onto each other they rolled and Drew ended up on top, gripping the man's throat with his left hand. The man was fighting for breath. His nose was bleeding like a tap and his hands grasped Drew's left arm to stop him being choked.

Although Drew did not recognise the man immediately, for a fraction of a second he thought he had seen him somewhere before. He heard more footsteps running towards him from the car, more 'hostiles.' There was no time to lose. Drew had to finish with the man on the ground, before he could turn and face the new threat.

In his days as a young soldier he remembered being told that, 'You cannot train a chin to take a punch.' That saying had helped him finish a few scraps by knocking out an aggressor with a hook to the chin. Drew thought, time for night-night mate. He drew his right arm back for a haymaker of a punch, when he heard a sound which stopped him dead.

A metallic racking sound from behind was either a pump-action shotgun loading a round into the chamber, or a friction-lock baton being extended, ready to cleave his skull open like a 'dippy egg.'

He froze with his right fist in the air, as a woman shouted, "Stop! *Señor Mayam.* Stop!"

A woman stood ready with a baton to strike him. She meant business. Drew was in an impossible position. He lifted both his hands up and recalled where he had seen the hostile man, and the woman, before - they were the suspicious looking couple at the café in Tosantos from a few days ago.

"They're on our side Drew!" shouted John as he climbed out of the back of the Seat Ibiza. "They're with us. Stop pissing about with Juan and get in the car, *Ouballie*."

Drew remembered that he was still on top of the man with the broken nose. He was making a growling noise and muttering, "*Bastardo!*"

Isabella put away her baton and helped Drew up. John found a first aid kit in the car and offered Juan a dressing to staunch the bleeding. Isabella reprimanded Juan for being reckless by running at *Señor Mayam* from behind. Drew apologised, but Juan just glared at him. The broken nose made Juan's eyes water heavily. He held a bandage to his nose.

Isabella took over the driving duties. "We need to get out of here before we attract too much attention," she said. Down the track there were several pilgrims heading towards them. Drew squeezed his rucksack into the boot of the car and sat in the front passenger seat. John sat with Juan in the back.

"The convent has space for you two tonight," said Isabella, driving them through Carrión, passing pilgrims who were wandering about. "*Señor* Dickinson, The Chief, is expecting a call from you later to brief you."

❖ ❖ ❖

The former convent, Albergue de las Religiosas Filipenses in Carrión, was so tranquil Drew found it surreal compared to the drama of the last few hours. Isabella had dropped Drew and John at the door and had driven Juan to have his broken nose treated.

Drew and John were greeted by a kindly old nun. John booked them both in. He took on Drew's role of managing the laundry by asking the nun if she would wash their clothes.

Drew had still not quite recovered from the effects of the spiked drink. Provided he was not dreaming he was relieved to see John and, it appeared, John was still in one piece.

If Drew had ever had a more refreshing shower, he could not remember it. Afterwards, he got changed and sat down with John in a common room in the *albergue*.

John explained what had happened after he and Davie left him earlier at Villalcázar de Sirga. Davie had been buzzing with excitement. John had seen this behaviour before, like a junkie getting strung out ready for his fix. John had a gut feeling that things were not right.

When they arrived in Carrión, Davie did not meet the keyholder for the AirBnB as he had stated. Apparently Davie already knew the code for the key box on the wall. John was convinced that Davie was not *kosher.* He had sat John down at a bar to wait for him to get the house ready. He said he had to go to a supermarket to get supplies.

It was while John was waiting at the bar on his own that Isabella casually approached him. She showed him a letter from Peter Dickinson, 'To whom it may concern.' The letter vouched that Isabella was working on behalf of the De Witt business.

Isabella said to John, "You are in the gravest of danger. Where is *Señor* Anderson?"

John explained that Davie was shopping and pointed out the AirBnB house. Isabella took John to the little car and was introduced to the driver, Juan.

Isabella rang officers from the *Policia Nacional* and issued them with instructions. It appeared that the police unit had already been mobilised and were waiting for the orders to execute some sort of raid. It also sounded like Isabella had considerable influence with the *Policia Nacional* and ordered them to storm the AirBnB place, *rapido.*

Davie had arrived back at the AirBnB house from the hardware store with masking tape, plastic sheeting, rope and a selection of knives. Before the police entered the house, Davie had time to quickly dress the bathroom with the plastic sheeting which was going to be his video studio, torture chamber and kill room. All to be live-streamed on the dark web for the viewing pleasure of a discrete number of sick individuals with crypto currency to burn.

When the *Policia Nacional* unit burst into the house and arrested Davie they discovered a large amount of illegal drugs. Davie resisted arrest and assaulted one of the police officers.

"This is about all I know. I will leave you to speak with Pete, I'm off to see a nun about our washing," said John, as he left the common room.

Drew started a video call with Dixie.

"What a day, matey?" said Peter, looking as happy as the cat that got the cream.

"Turned out nice again... I think. John has given me the basics," said Drew.

"Okay. Where to begin? I suppose the first thing to say is that everyone is very relieved that the threat posed by Davie Anderson has been neutralised. Paul de Witt is delighted. He wished to pass on his thanks to you. And you have met our local extraction team, Isabella and Juan," said Peter.

"Yes, it was a surprise to me. I didn't know who they were. You could have told me about them, Dixie," said Drew, a little annoyed.

"It was a surprise to Juan, so I'm told. I heard you gave him a 'Liverpool kiss,'" said Peter, grinning widely.

"Oh, the headbutt. I was still a bit confused and I took him for a hostile," said Drew, slightly embarrassed.

"Well he's bloody hostile now!" said Peter, laughing. "Not exactly Queensbury rules, me old china."

"Wouldn't have headbutted him had I known he was on our side," said Drew, trying to justify himself.

"Ah well, lesson learned. Anyway, what do you think of Isabella?" asked Peter.

"Very professional. I'm well impressed," said Drew.

"Agreed," said Peter. "Isabella was a big loss to the *Policia Nacional* when she went to the private security world. Still has lots of contacts in Spanish law enforcement," Drew concluded he knew where Dixie was getting his insider information from. "She is top class. This type of job is small beer to her. She's a bit like a thoroughbred racehorse giving donkey rides."

"What's happened to Davie?"

"Once the *Policia Nacional* raided the AirBnB house they found drugs. Lots of them. A dealer quantity of cocaine as well as a 'party pack' of other substances, like the valium I think he used to spike your water bottle.

"The police assumed that the plastic sheeted bathroom was going to an illegal drugs lab. This supports them to charge Davie with possession of drugs with intent to supply. Of course we know what Davie was really planning to do in the room," said Peter.

"John said he assaulted one of the cops."

"Assaulted? Try, slashed across the neck with a scalpel! Luckily it wasn't deep enough to be life threatening, but Davie could be charged with the attempted murder of a *Policia Nacional* officer, not just a wounding.

"The police also found Davie had two other passports, in different names. From initial inquiries the police reckon he was born in South Africa to Scottish parents. More than that they don't yet know.

"Interpol will be trying to find undetected crimes related to the other aliases in his forged passports. He is likely to be on remand for months and imprisoned for years. I will be well into retirement before Davie ever tastes freedom again. Guess what has not happened to Davie's probation officer?" asked Peter.

"I dunno," said Drew, a little confused.

"Davie's probation officer hasn't been born yet! That will teach Davie not to fart in church," Peter laughed at his own humour.

Drew was puzzled that Peter was not pressing for Davie to be prosecuted for stalking John. Peter said that the information from the dark web was unlikely to be of evidential value. Drew speculated that maybe some of Peter's investigation methods would not meet the highest ethical standards demanded of the criminal justice system.

"Anyway, our VIPs don't want to appear in court as victims for years to come. It is only likely to increase interest in them, possibly inspire copycats. This way, Davie will spend months on remand for the cocaine, setting up a drugs lab, slashing the police officer and whatever Interpol can link him to from the false passports. He will have a charge sheet longer than a docker's tea break," explained Peter. "It is what I'd call a 'Good Result.'"

"I'm so relieved that John is unscathed."

"We can't let our guard down, but I think we can breathe a bit easier tonight, matey," said Peter. "And the best news of all is that I have been summoned to a meeting with our Human Resources director."

"And that's a good thing?" said Drew, sceptically.

"Definitely. I asked for my salary and reward package to be reviewed months ago, so I have been waiting for a meeting with HR for some time. I'm expecting big things, matey. I'll update you in a day or so," Peter said with a huge grin on his face.

"Hope you will remember the little people, like me, when you become mega wealthy," said Drew.

"Who are you again?" said Peter, still smiling as he ended the video meeting.

◆ ◆ ◆

Drew and John attended the 6 pm mass at the Iglesia de Santa Maria del Camino.

At the end of the service the priest invited the twenty or so pilgrims to come forward for a blessing. One of The Young Crowd, Siobhán, limped to the altar to translate the priest's address into English for the pilgrims.

A pilgrim association volunteer also joined in and asked Siobhán to translate for him as well. The informality between the two men and Siobhán, as well as other pilgrims chipping in their suggestions for alternative translations, was entertaining and contrasted with the solemnity of the mass which had just ended.

Siobhán, and her young cohort, truly embodied the positive spirit of the *Camino*.

◆ ◆ ◆

On leaving the church, Drew and John drifted back towards their accommodation. They passed the Plaza de la Constitución and heard the throbbing music from the disco bar.

The pair stopped at a table outside Restaurant Naturale for dinner. Drew chose a bowl of sautéed fresh vegetables instead of the juicy steak which John ate.

"John, I'm just so relieved everything worked out so well in the end today," said Drew, his relief was palpable.

"Me too," said John, finishing his plate. "Fancy popping into the disco bar to embrace the local culture?"

They deserved to let their hair down. On the Plaza, the disco bar emitted a heavy bass beat from the live band. Like moths to a flame the pair went in.

The dark crowded bar spilled onto an equally crowded dance floor in front of the band. As well as couples, a young woman was in front of the band dancing a sensual routine which mesmerised everyone who looked at her. She saw Drew's young companion, smiled and beckoned him to join her with a come hither tilt of her head, under her NY Yankees baseball cap.

John sidled up to Ellen and they moved as if they had known each other forever. They danced passionately and kissed, oblivious to what was going on around them.

The band had finished their set and left the stage. The lights had come up. The dance floor cleared. Ellen and John were still locked in an embrace. Eventually they sensed they were alone and shuffled self-consciously off the dance floor.

"Hiya... Mister Bodyguard," said Ellen to Drew. She was drunk.

John helped Ellen to her hostal only a short stagger from the bar. He rejoined Drew and they rushed back to the convent before it closed its doors for the night.

Drew felt a glow of satisfaction that John had been responsible, looked after Ellen and not got drunk himself, for once.

21. CARRIÓN TO TERRADILLOS

<u>400 km to Santiago de Compostela.</u>

Drew woke early. Yesterday was successful, but he knew it was a close run thing. Amanda, Davie Anderson, would be waking up in a Spanish prison cell. He was no longer a problem, but there was always the 'unknown unknown' or 'Black Swan' threat; so it was time to switch on and get a grip.

John was up and ready when Drew left his room. They each had two litres of water with them. Today's first leg to the nearest village was going to be 17 km. No stops, shops, cafés, bars or water fountains. *Nada.*

"Okay, Romeo. Let's walk," whispered Drew with a smile and they crept out of the *albergue* just after 6.30 am. The pair walked through Carrión de los Condes in the dark. They soon left the slumbering town and were out onto the *Meseta.* Moonlight provided enough illumination for them to not need a head torch.

◆ ◆ ◆

Dawn broke after about an hour or so. The sun came up like a searchlight and its warm embrace was welcome. The moon had still not set.

"I forgot to ask you how last night's meeting went with Uncle Pete," said John.

"Never seen him happier. He was relieved that Davie will be eating Spanish prison food for many decades to come. He was even looking forward to a meeting last night with the head of HR," said Drew.

"Really?" exclaimed John.

"Yes. I expect him to brag later that his salary has been bumped up. The last time I saw him so happy was years ago when we were in the army and he was promoted to sergeant after his tour in Northern Ireland," said Drew.

"Was that the time he was blown up, but still managed to drag you all the way back to safety under a hail of heavy machine-gun fire?" asked John.

"Yeah, it was something like that," said Drew, recalling that awful day in Belfast and lying wounded in the rain, next to the body of the dead policewoman covered with a green army poncho. John noticed that Drew walked with a slight limp.

"What's wrong with your foot, *Ouballie*?" asked John.

"Oh nothing. Just Mister Blister saying 'hello' on my toe," said Drew.

John insisted that they stop and check it out. There was something in John's tone which Drew took to be an instruction, rather than a polite suggestion. They stopped.

As John drained Drew's blister and taped it up, Drew reflected on how far they had come. Not just in kilometres walked, but on the journey of life.

"Thank you, partner. Let's walk," said Drew.

The trail was arrow straight. The fields stretched to the horizon. Occasionally the pair met with other pilgrims like Frank, a 72 year old widower from New York. He had planned to walk the *Camino* with his wife. Now he walked The Way with the spirit of his wife in his heart.

Bonnie, a fast Australian from Perth, swished past.

Lots of noisy *Bicigrinos* from Mexico rattled along. They were on an organised tour with their own van and bike trailer.

The pair caught up with eight women pilgrims all happily conversing in Spanish. They all left the track at the same time to find bushes that were in urgent need of watering. Drew concluded that it was not just in pubs and restaurants that women go to the toilets together. They do it in the wild as well, but he did not have a clue as to why. The *Camino* was littered with used tissues. Drew decided that if toilets were provided at regular intervals this would not be the case.

Calzadilla de la Cueza was the first village after 17 km from Carrión de los Condes. Bonnie was having a break outside a café with a couple of other pilgrims.

Drew and John decided to simply refill their

water bottles at the fountain and press on through Calzadilla de la Cueza, in spite of a confusion of painted arrows on the roads. The arrows directed pilgrims away from the official route, to the economic advantage of local bar owners.

♦ ♦ ♦

Another hour and a half brought the pair to Ledigos.

At bar La Morena they stopped for a 'boots off' break, *café cortados* and *Neapolitanas.* They were joined by Martin, a Dutch former-artilleryman, James (one of The Young Crowd) from Oxford, Bonnie the fleet of foot Aussie cardiac nurse, another Martin from the Netherlands they had met in Belorado, and Lena, the Japanese woman they last saw in the *albergue* in Castrojeriz. They shared stories about their *Camino* experiences. John decided not to tell them about his close encounter with Davie, his psychopath stalker.

As they were about to leave, Drew asked for *dos café con leche para llevar* from the bar. He put his rucksack on, donned his hat and carefully balanced both disposable coffee cups on top of each other, as he headed out.

"You go on, John," Drew said. "I've just got to say 'hi' to a couple of old friends."

In the road outside bar La Morena, Drew went up to the passenger side of a Seat Ibiza and said, "*Hola Amiga,*" at Isabella who was acting casually.

She opened the window.

"Thought you might need a hot drink or two," as he handed her the coffees. He reached into his pocket, brought out some sachets of sugar and a couple of wooden stirrers.

"*Gracias*," Isabella said, flatly.

"*Buenos dias, Amigo*," Drew said to Juan who looked straight ahead, not acknowledging his presence.

Drew felt he had caused the pair enough embarrassment and started to walk after John.

He presumed that parking so blatantly outside the bar was probably not Isabella's idea and imagined she was going to verbally bust Juan's balls later.

"What was that all about Drew?" said John.

"Those two clowns, Isabella and Juan, were parked outside the bar, so I thought I'd have a bit of fun and give them something to drink," said Drew. "Covert surveillance? They're a joke."

"Don't you think that's the dumbest place to be parked, if they were trying to be clandestine?" said John. "I mean they can't be that stupid."

"What's on your mind?" Drew asked.

"Maybe their orders are different now. Before, they were part of the extraction plan to get me to a place of safety. Do you think that Pete has now told them to be a little more obvious? Maybe the security risk has changed. Has he mentioned anything like this to you?"

"Dixie didn't mention any changes in the risk

environment when I spoke with him last night."

John was surprised, "That's odd, man."

"I think you could be right. Maybe Isabella's assignment instructions have been changed. I will ask Dixie about it when I speak to him at six."

22. TERRADILLOS DE LA TEMPLARIOS

In the third village that the pair came to that day, Terradillos de la Templarios, they stopped at the Albergue Jacques de Molay. The *albergue* had bunks and also provided a dinner.

Once they had settled in, showered and were resting on their bunks in the empty dormitory Drew said, "Do you know who Jacques de Molay was?"

"The guy who owns this hostel," said John.

"Not exactly," Drew chuckled. "He was grandmaster of the Knights Templar. The warrior monk types who protected pilgrims. They were such an influential and wealthy organisation that the French King Philip moved against him, and the rest of the Templars in the thirteen hundreds on Friday the thirteenth. It didn't end well for Jacques."

"Is that how you see yourself? A warrior monk protecting me," asked John.

"In a way perhaps I am. Anyway I have been wanting to ask you. Are you comfortable talking about what happened in the Caribbean?"

"*Ja*, no problem. What do you want to know?"

said John.

"I mean it must have been most distressing, but please talk me through it."

John explained that he had gone to Tobago against Peter Dickinson's advice. It was almost a spur of the moment decision to go, so in theory very few people were privy to his travel plans. He told Drew that he had been abducted on his very first night by a team of three kidnappers who knew who he was. How the gang were furnished with the information about him was a mystery. He did not feel that they were master criminals, more like foot soldiers. The more John pondered the issue, the more he believed that someone in the travel agency, or the resort, or, God forbid, inside De Witt's leaked his itinerary. It was like a military operation and the gang adhered to a plan. By luck, Peter was in the right place at the right time in Florida. He worked with the security consultants and operated from the De Witt regional office in Miami.

"There were some oddities that still niggle me," said John, pensively.

"What oddities were they?"

"Firstly, and this is just maybe a minor thing," said John. "One of the kidnappers called his machete a 'cutlass.' It would have been amusing had it not been razor sharp and held against my throat at the time. Like something from a Pirates of the Caribbean film. I didn't know that Trinidadians call their machetes 'cutlasses,' but

Pete did."

"How did he know?"

"He said that when he was in the UK he trained soldiers from the Trinidad and Tobago regiment and heard them use the word," said John.

"Interesting, what else?" asked Drew, increasingly suspicious about the abduction.

"One of the threats the kidnappers used, to put pressure on the family to pay up, was they were going to castrate me," said John, in a matter of fact way.

"Ouch!"

"Now they could have used any type of threat, but I specifically overheard the gang say they were going to cut my balls off. That has special relevance to the inheritance of the money held in trust for my offspring. No balls equals no kids, which means big problems. It was as if the gang knew exactly what to say to get attention from the company. It could have been luck that the gang used that threat, but I'm not so sure."

Drew did not like coincidences either. "Anything else?" he asked.

"Well the big question is how did the police know the location to mount a rescue? And, thinking about it, why were they not brought into the confidence of the family?" John asked, rhetorically.

"So the local cops weren't made aware of the kidnapping?" asked Drew, somewhat surprised.

"No. Pete said that the consultants advised

him to brief the police, but he said that the Board overruled him. I'm not happy with that," said John.

"Why?"

"The Board are scared of their own shadows. We'd say they were *bangbroek*. Not involving the police is a risky thing to do. That's not the kind of decision they are likely to make, they are risk averse in the extreme. I only have Pete's word that the Board didn't want the police informed," said John.

"It must have been a surprise for the SWAT to find you in the gang's hideout."

"More than a surprise. A bloody shock!" exclaimed John, reliving the incident. "They're shooting the gang members with twenty rounds of rapid fire and I'm on the floor with my hands up, *kaking* myself."

"You'd wonder how the police found out where the gang were."

"It might have been dumb luck," said John, "but I can't help thinking it was a 'mischievous' tip off."

"Why do you say 'mischievous?'"

"The police seemed convinced that the gang were armed with AK47 assault rifles, as if whoever tipped them off wanted the police to go in hard and slot them."

Drew pondered, "You've got to ask yourself, 'Who benefits?'"

"I hate to think like this, and maybe I shouldn't say it," said John, somberly.

"Just say it."

"There is only one person who knew my itinerary; probably had contacts with local former soldiers; knew the financial implications of castrating me; and could influence the Board into not involving the police," said John, then paused, "Pete Dickinson."

Drew exhaled, before saying, "If Dixie was the 'fourth man' he would know your location and know just the right time in the kidnap operation for the police to strike. Just after the ransom had been paid and before you were released. And if he tipped off the police and upped the ante by saying they had machine-guns, the storming would be likely to lead to the elimination of the gang. I hate to say it, but I think you're right." Drew did not want to believe where the facts had led them.

"Then this latest problem with Davie," said John.

"Some of the information Dixie has given me makes me suspect he has people working within law enforcement," said Drew, thinking that Isabella could be his intelligence source.

"Makes me question who I can trust," said John.

"I feel the same myself," said Drew. "Don't think I should come right out and challenge Dixie at my six o'clock meeting. He keeps on telling me that I'm in his 'Circle of Trust.'"

"The question is, do you trust Pete?" asked John.

Drew told John that they had to rely on each

other. If all else failed they always had the safety net of making a call to Paul de Witt.

"*Ja*, but let's see if we can be grown-ups here and survive on our own, eh," said John.

◆ ◆ ◆

At 6 pm Drew started the video meeting and waited for Peter to connect. And waited. And waited. "Come on Dixie, don't ghost me now man," muttered Drew, before the session timed out.

He tried Peter's mobile number, but this rang and went to a recorded message on voicemail, "You're through to Peter's phone. You know the drill," then a tone. "Hello Dixie it's Drew. Where are you? Call me back."

Options? thought Drew. The standard communication plan was for them to hold a daily sitrep at 6 pm by video. In exceptional circumstances they could contact each other directly. Maybe Drew should do nothing and try again tomorrow.

Drew thought about getting Paul de Witt's number from John and contacting him, but if Peter was just tied up with another security task, it would seem unnecessary to bother Paul. Damn it.

Drew decided to make a contact call with the Global Security Operations Centre and get them to let Peter know everything was OK.

Drew dialled the GSOC with the international prefix +27. The call was answered promptly, "Good evening. Security. How may I help?" said an efficient sounding South African male voice.

"Hello. This is Nursemaid. I'd like to leave a message for Peter Dickinson," said Drew.

After a short pause, "Who is this?"

"Nursemaid."

"Who?" said the security officer.

"It's my codename. Nursemaid. Peter told me that if I said the name you'd know I was genuine," said Drew, feeling slightly absurd.

"Is this some kind of a joke man?" asked security.

"No, okay. Can I leave a message for Peter Dickinson? Tell him to call Nurse-, no tell him to call Andrew Mallam. Can you do that for me?"

"What is your number?" asked security.

"Peter, knows my number."

"Mr Dickinson is not," the security officer paused, "Mr Dickinson is not available at the moment. Please may I have your number?"

"It's okay. Leave it. I will speak to him tomorrow," said Drew and he was about to hang up.

"Ah! Nursemaid!" said the security officer with a positive tone.

"Er, yes. Correct, that's my codename."

"Ah yes. I have just found the trigger plan for the operation you are on," said security.

"Phew! That's great. Now may I speak with Peter?" said Drew, very relieved.

"That's still not possible at the present

moment in time," said security.

"Why not?"

"I am not at liberty to say," said the officer, in a scripted way.

Bloody security thought Drew, "Okay, well may I leave him a message?"

"Certainly. What is your message please?" asked security.

"Oi Dixie! call me back you bastard. End of message."

"Okay. I will read it back to you, 'Peter please call me.'" said the security officer, diplomatically.

"Yeah I suppose that'll do. Goodbye," said Drew and he hung up.

❖ ❖ ❖

At dinner Drew and John were joined by a British couple, Daniel and Liz, as well as Frank from New York.

Drew chose the lentil soup followed by the chicken in a *bravas* sauce.

Frank asked Daniel, "Have you done other *Caminos*?"

While Daniel was rattling off the various *Caminos* he had walked, Drew just listened. He was not scintillating company that night, he was annoyed that Dixie had been a no-show. Luckily Frank and Daniel were great conversationalists. John pitched in with extolling the welcome they had received from the nuns in Carrión. Nobody bothered asking Drew why he was in such a bad mood.

Frank tried to convince Daniel that the *Camino* had given him a fresh perspective on the environmental crisis and extolled the virtues of a green economy. Daniel was checking his phone, "Frank, let's assume you flew here from the States economy class, that's one tonne of CO2. Double it if you are flying back. Tell me again about this green stuff you are talking about, pal?"

At the end of the meal, Drew stood up stiffly and wished his dinner partners, *"Buenas noches."*

He went back to the dormitory. John followed a few minutes later.

"In a rush to leave the table *Ouballie*?" asked John.

"Oh the conversation was about to go downhill," replied Drew.

John laughed, "You're right. Frank was trying to take the moral high ground saying we should all give up on fossil fuels, 'Beethoven didn't need all this tech to write his music' and all that stuff. With Dan accusing him of being part of the problem by flying to Spain when he could walk the Appalachian Trail from his home."

"Sorry I was in a mood tonight, John," said Drew, apologetically. "Pete didn't show up on the video call, so I left him a message with his security team. Expect he will leave me a message soon. Probably been celebrating a massive increase in his pay packet after his meeting with HR."

"I thought you were grinding your teeth when Dan was bragging about the number of *Caminos* he has walked. Back home we'd say you were *dikbek,* you grumpy *Ouballie,*" replied John, settling into his bunk.

"You noticed," Drew laughed. "It was the way Daniel said he 'did' so many *Caminos,* not 'walked' *Caminos.* What does it mean to 'do' a *Camino*? In Scotland there are nearly three hundred mountains over three thousand feet. They are called Munros and there are mountaineers who spend their life 'bagging-Munros.' What's the point? Does it mean anything?"

John laughed, "Which bloody question do you want me to bloody answer? Get some sleep Drew. You will feel better in the bloody morning."

"Yeah, good plan. Goodnight John."

About an hour later The Young Crowd came into the dormitory. Getting some sleep was not high on their agenda.

Yet again, Drew fumbled around for his ear plugs.

23. TERRADILLOS TO SAHAGÚN

<u>374 km to Santiago de Compostela.</u>

The pair started from Terradillos de la Templarios before 7 am. Another moonlit walk on farm tracks without the need for a head torch. The sky was lit with countless stars.

Out of habit Drew identified Polaris, The Pole Star, by the constellations of Ursa Major, The Plough, and Cassiopeia. By establishing that north was on his right he was reassured that he was heading due west. Christian pilgrims would have done the same for a thousand years. Before that, so too would pagans.

Drew scoured the night sky for The Pleiades, or Seven Sisters, cluster. He could not find it. Maybe it was the wrong time of year. So many old cultures have stories about such stars. Maybe the ancients were just trying to make sense of the universe, he thought.

The Way came to a T-junction with an official left turn sign onto a track parallel with the road. After 100 metres the track ran out. There was no other signage. They were forced to walk on the asphalt surface, in the dark. Drew switched on his head torch for the benefit of drivers on the road. The pair carried straight on. After an anxious few minutes another official sign directed them to the right onto another track through a forest.

◆ ◆ ◆

Whilst going through Moratinos they were joined by two Aussie *peregrinas*, Polly and Sally. They all stopped for breakfast of coffee and a really large portion of *tortilla patatas* at Restaurante Casa Barrunta in San Nicolás del Real Camino.

While they were eating John announced that, according to his phone, San Nicolás del Real Camino's claim to fame was that it was the official halfway point on the *Camino Frances*.

"Wow! So we are halfway from Saint-Jean-Pied-de-Port to Santiago de Compostela?" said Polly.

"Er... No. About halfway between Roncesvalles and Santiago," said John.

"Hang on," said Sally, incredulously. "You mean that the *Camino Frances* in Spain 'officially' starts in Roncesvalles, rather than Saint-Jean?"

"There may be some argument about it, but 'yes' it would appear so," said John.

"Wish I'd known that before I climbed the damn Pyrenees from Saint-Jean on that awful first day. It was a crippler!" said Sally, laughing.

All the pilgrims saw the funny side of this

news. The Aussie women were great company.

The sun had risen and it was time to go on the last few kilometres into Sahagún. And it started to rain steadily. The pilgrims covered their rucksacks and put their waterproofs on. The wind picked up and there was no shelter, as the trail was alongside the main road.

Up ahead, Drew and John saw an elderly pilgrim walking ponderously slowly. He had a massive rucksack and was just wearing trousers and a shirt. No jacket, anorak or poncho to protect him. He was soaked to the skin. Several other pilgrims had passed the old man without pausing.

When John got alongside the man he asked him if he could do anything to help him. To the old man, John was a virtual lifesaver. Drew observed John being a Good Samaritan. The old man was a German in his mid-80s. He could not take his poncho from his rucksack and put it on, without considerable help. John insisted he stop so he could get the poncho out and fit it over him and his backpack.

Drew asked the German if he had eaten, "*Hast du gegessen?*"

He shook his head. Drew got a cereal bar from his side pouch, "*Bitte essen.*"

Drew and John made sure their fellow pilgrim was well covered by his poncho, eating the snack and walking on.

Drew and John continued towards Sahagún which was now in sight. Every few minutes John turned around to make sure the German guy was still plodding on steadily.

"I'm impressed, John. I don't think the guy would have died of hypothermia, but you certainly made his trek a lot more comfortable."

"Thanks, Drew. It is what you would have done," said John.

"Oh, yes. However, we saw lots of pilgrims ignore the guy, although they could clearly see he was struggling. Well done," said Drew, as he gave John a friendly slap on the shoulder.

"Where did you learn German?" asked John.

"A long time ago I served in Germany in the British army. The first phrase I learnt was, *'Zwei Bier. Mein Freund zahlt.'*"

"What's that mean?" asked John.

"Two beers. My friend is paying."

24. SAHAGÚN

The pair arrived in Sahagún. Drew checked his phone for messages, Dixie had still to make contact. They were a little early to check into an *albergue* and Drew needed a pharmacy. An insect had bitten his left hand on the way from Fromista to Carrión and it had swollen up like a catcher's mitt. At a *farmacia* he received the professional advice he was after and anti-histamine cream.

The two men arrived at Albergue de Peregrinos Cluny, booked in and claimed their bunk beds. They went through their usual routine - showered and did their laundry before they started some traditional afternoon sleeping.

❖ ❖ ❖

After an hour, Drew had a guest, escorted to the dormitory by the *hospitalera*.

"*Buenas tardes, Meester Mayam,*" said Juan, with barely concealed menace. "You to come with me. *Por favor.*"

"And John?" asked Drew, admiring the blue-grey bruising spreading around both of Juan's eyes from his broken nose.

"*Solo,*" said Juan, "Meeting. *Muy importante.*" At last, thought Drew, finally I can get to speak to

Dixie.

"My date has arrived. A meeting with Peter I presume. Don't wait up," Drew said to John, who was relaxing on his bunk.

"Okay. Drew, don't do anything I wouldn't do. And be back before midnight or you'll turn into a pumpkin," said John, cheekily.

◆ ◆ ◆

Drew got into the Seat Ibiza and was excited to be travelling faster than walking pace again. Much faster. Juan did not speak to Drew at all. The atmosphere was 'frosty'.

Juan parked at the Hotel Puerta de Sahagún. He took Drew into a business meeting room, where Isabella was sitting with her laptop computer open.

"*Señor* Gourney, here is Mister Mayam now," she got up and invited Drew to sit down looking at the screen.

Drew had expected to see Peter Dickinson, but instead saw a conference room setup with one person in shot at the table. A thin faced, balding, middle-aged man with rectangular frameless spectacles. He wore a ubiquitous blue business suit jacket over a plain white shirt, without a tie. On the table was a typed briefing note and a glass of water.

"Hello Mr Mallam. I'm Xavier Gourney, European General Manager for De Witt's. This is in the strictest confidence. I am based in Paris and, regrettably, cannot meet with you in person." Through the windows of the conference room Drew saw a skyline typical of Paris. He half expected to see the *Eiffel Tower* or *Arc de Triomphe*.

"I hope I can be assured of your utmost discretion in what I'm about to discuss with you," said Xavier.

"Before you go any further, may I ask why Peter Dickinson isn't here? I was expecting to see him," said Drew.

"You put me in a most difficult position Andrew," said Xavier, taking a sip of water, "I will tell you now because you will hear about it eventually. Please prepare yourself for bad news. With deepest regret, I have to tell you that Peter has... taken his life."

"What! No way. You've gotta be kidding me," Drew gripped the arms of the chair, as he felt like the room might spin.

"I would not make a joke out of such a tragedy. Please accept my condolences, I am aware you were former comrades."

"Oh good God. That's bloody devastating. I can hardly take it in. Do you know why?"

"I'm sure you have a thousand questions," said Xavier, adjusting his glasses and checking his briefing note, "but firstly I must establish the professional relationship between you and the company. Have you had any written contract for protective services from us?" Drew got the feeling that there may have been more people around the conference table out of view. Possibly a minute taker and someone from human resources or maybe a legal adviser. Drew looked at the office windows behind Xavier, to see if there were reflections of others in the room, but the glass gave nothing away.

"I think you know the answer to that. No, I refused to be bound by a contract, it was a handshake between Peter and myself," said Drew, trying to make sense of what was happening.

Xavier breathed a slight sigh of relief, as if Drew's answer fitted with his own understanding of the situation. Drew was still stunned by the tragic news and even thought, was this some sort of sick joke dreamt up by Dixie?

"Were you given anything by Peter?" asked Xavier.

Drew was starting to marshal his thoughts, "I'm assuming you have access to Peter's emails, so you'll know I have personal information packages relating to John and I have a cash card for expenses."

"Thank you, Andrew. Were you given any other financial reward or promise of reward?" asked Xavier, ticking another item from the checklist in front of him.

"Dixi- I mean Peter said that he would provide me with a lump sum equivalent to a thousand pounds a day, as a consultancy fee at the end of the assignment," said Drew. "In cash."

Xavier appeared slightly surprised and said, "Andrew, I have to say Peter had no authority to make any such promise."

"I wasn't holding my breath actually," scoffed Drew. "Can you give me more information about Peter's death? I mean, did he leave a note?"

"What I can say, is that the catalyst appears to have been the emergence of a video tape from the archive of an American cameraman. He was tasked by PIRA to film one of their terrorist attacks in West Belfast in 1983," said Xavier, drinking more water. "The cameraman died recently and his old video came to light. PIRA had thought that all the copies of the tape were destroyed as, let's say, it did not cover them in any glory and, on balance, they thought it would negatively affect support for their 'cause.' Did you know that the incident, where Peter allegedly rescued you, was filmed?"

"No. This is news to me. Do you have access to the film?" asked Drew, more than a little surprised that a video had emerged from the mists of time. And puzzled further by Xavier's use of the word 'allegedly.'

"I thought you might ask for that," Xavier paused, "I am prepared to play it for you, but I must warn you that what you will see is... shocking."

Drew gulped and just said, "Play it."

Xavier shared his screen with Isabella's laptop, which showed a still image of a derelict house on a rainy street in Belfast. The video started.

A soldier could be seen to look from an

alleyway a couple of times before dashing out to take up a position in front of the boarded-up house. The soldier looked up and down the street as if he was perplexed. A second soldier appeared from the alleyway and took up a position on the corner, when the house exploded. The camera shook and an American accent was heard to say, "Jesus H Christ!"

The street was a mass of debris, dust, smoke and car alarms. Before the dust settled the microphone picked up crack-thump, crack-thump, crack-thump of a high velocity rifle being fired in the street.

Through the dust a policewoman appeared to remonstrate with the soldier at the corner of the street by the alleyway. As the view became clearer, the body of the first soldier was seen lying motionless among the bricks and other debris on the pavement.

The video and Drew's own sketchy memory were both in agreement, thus far.

The camera then caught an incident of incredible bravery, as the policewoman ran to the fallen soldier and tried again and again to drag him around the pile of debris to safety.

Drew looked puzzled and shook his head as he watched the action unfold. Surely, some clever video fakery or artifice was being played out here, he assumed.

All the time crack-thump, crack-thump was heard. In the final effort to drag the unresponsive soldier behind cover, thud-thump. It appeared that the policewoman was felled by an invisible sledgehammer and flopped backwards onto the cowering soldier.

Although Drew knew the fatal shot was coming, it still startled him.

On the video, a truck engine was heard accelerating hard. The crouching soldier became animated, it looked like he used his radio and was joined by a third soldier from the alleyway, carrying a large radio-type device on his back.

"Oh Dixie! You stupid tosser!" said Drew under his breath, shaking his head. He was scarcely able to comprehend what he just saw. His heart raced and perspiration ran down his face, he felt as if he had been poleaxed. Everything he had been led to believe for decades, had been a lie.

The screen reverted back to the conference room. "You can appreciate that Peter's professional integrity had been compromised by this video," said Xavier, in an undemonstrative way. "In his note, he requested that his medals be returned and asked for forgiveness from the police officer's family for stealing her valour."

"So. What happens next?" asked Drew, he tried to calm his breathing, still in a state of mild shock.

"There are so many loose ends to tie up. Our Communications department is handling press releases and the media strategy-"

"More importantly, what happens with John?" interrupted Drew.

Xavier looked slightly nervous and glanced off camera.

"Your help is most appreciated by the family and we will arrange for John to be exfiltrated. I think that is the correct security term. A modest *ex-gratia* payment has been authorised in return for a non-disclosure agreement on your part," another item from Xavier's checklist ticked off. It sounded to Drew that Xavier was working from a script which had been drafted by his HR director.

"It's all about money with you people. I ain't signing any gagging clause and you can have no worries about my discretion. My lips are sealed.

"I will be walking the *Camino* to Santiago tomorrow with John," said Drew, feeling that he was about to lose his temper.

"I am afraid that is no longer an option. Juan, who I believe you have met," Xavier stroked his nose and Drew would swear that he detected a half-smile, "is escorting John right now to the hotel you are in, as a temporary measure. We will be responsible for his protection from here on. He will remain in Sahagún until a flight is arranged to bring him home, hopefully tomorrow."

"So I'm being stood down?"

"If that is the way you wish to put it, yes. I will ask that you hand over the cash card to Isabella and allow her to witness you deleting the documents you received from the late Peter Dickinson from your phone. I thank you for your assistance so far and I hope I can rely on your continued discretion in this most delicate of situations," said Xavier, in a business-like tone and finished with, "*Muchas gracias,* Isabella."

The video conference session ended and the laptop reverted to a screen saver. Drew noticed that Isabella had a printed document in duplicate, which he had been expected to sign. He gave her the cash card, deleted the personal information file from his phone and she watched him while he also emptied the phone's trash folder.

They waited in the hotel for Juan to return to take Drew back to his more modest accommodation. Isabella broke the awkward silence and explained that she was the team leader from a Madrid based security company which had been contracted by Peter Dickinson. Their job was to intervene if necessary to extract John if there was a real and present threat to his security. Since Peter's death, Xavier had given them instructions to get closer to John until he got to Sahagún.

Drew got the impression that Isabella was the brains of the outfit; Juan the driver and muscle.

◆ ◆ ◆

Juan drove Drew in silence back to his *albergue.* Juan stopped the car and got out to say goodbye.

"*Adios amigo,*" said Drew offering Juan his hand. In a flash, Juan's left fist drove straight and hard into Drew's abdomen catching him off guard.

The punch to the *solar plexus* knocked the wind out of Drew, he doubled over unable to breathe. He felt a hammer blow punch to the left side of his head which floored him. Drew lay in the foetal position, with the taste of blood in his mouth and the world spinning.

Juan bent down and snarled into his ear, "*Adios Meester Mayam y Buen Camino!*"

Juan got back into the car and drove off, leaving Drew gasping for air. He heard footsteps approaching. A woman shouted, "Oh my God did you see that, Kym? Call the police, the robber is getting away."

Drew was in agony, but managed to get to his knees thinking, never stay down.

"Can you speak English?" said the woman with a London accent.

"Am... English," gasped Drew. "No cops," breath. "No police."

"You can't let these criminals get away with this," said the woman putting a caring arm around his shoulders.

"Long... story," said Drew. Unable to stand up fully unaided, he stretched and put his right hand on the woman's shoulder. "Please," was all he could manage to say.

The woman helped Drew into the reception area of the *albergue*, where he flopped onto a chair and the woman's friend joined them.

"Why did that awful man attack you?" asked the woman in a concerned voice.

"Oh I dunno," gasped Drew. "Maybe 'cos I broke his nose... a few days... ago."

"Honestly! The company you keep," the woman reprimanded Drew.

Drew stifled a laugh which caused a coughing spasm. "Thank you for... your concern," said Drew extending his hand, "I'm... Drew."

"Nice to meet you. I think," said the woman shaking his hand, "I'm Grace."

"Grace... you're... amazing," said Drew, still able to crack a joke.

"Do you need to see a doctor and get a check-up?" asked Grace's friend, Kym.

"I think... I will be alright... Just winded, is all."

"Did he knock you out?" asked Grace.

Drew touched the left side of his head. Juan's punch had caught him between his ear and eye. "Where there's no sense... there's no feeling. It is just sore... Just need to... lie down."

Drew made his way slowly to his bunk and lay on his right side. He thought, it's all over, just rest now.

◆ ◆ ◆

"Oi sleepyhead. Are you still with us?" said a woman's voice.

Drew slowly opened an eye and saw it was Grace and he said, "Did you get the number of the bus?"

"The number of what?" asked Grace.

"The bus that ran over me?" joked Drew.

"Funny man. Thought you could do with a drink," Grace said, offering Drew a bottle of mineral water and a blister pack of tablets, "and some painkillers."

"Ah. Just what I need," Drew said, as he slowly sat up with the world's biggest headache.

"Kym thinks it's not a good idea for you just to sleep after your bang to the head. She's a matron and takes no crap. Especially from men who go around busting other men's noses. We've decided to take you to dinner so we can monitor your vital signs. Burger okay for you?"

"Sounds simply divine," said Drew, groggily.

◆ ◆ ◆

Drew got up and shambled after Grace and Kym to a fast food outlet. He had become Their Project.

Matron Kym allowed Drew to drink more water and have a small ice-cream. He actually yearned for a massive burger and chips, like the women were munching their way through. When Kym was not looking Drew managed to steal several chips from Grace's tray.

Grace and Kym were both in their mid-50s. They appeared to be experienced and regular hikers. Drew told the women that he had a disagreement a couple of days ago with the man who beat him up outside the *albergue*. He made up a story that it was over the affection of a woman, which they appeared to believe.

Kym used the light on her phone to check for pupillary function in Drew's eyes and felt his pulse. She had short peroxide blonde hair, beautiful blue eyes and Drew felt an energy from her when she was checking his pulse. You are sexy to the tips of your fingers, he thought, but did not say it.

"You'll live," declared Kym, flatly. She looked at the left hand side of Drew's head where Juan had landed a haymaker of a punch.

"You've been in the wars. What the hell happened here?" asked Kym, as she ran her fingertips lightly over the numerous old tiny scars down Drew's face from his left temple to his jawline.

"Oh that serves me right for standing next to a bomb," said Drew, recalling the explosion back in Belfast.

"Dear Lord!" exclaimed Grace. "You're a magnet for trouble."

The overwhelming sense Drew felt was the kindness he received from these two sweet women.

◆ ◆ ◆

When they got back to the *albergue* later that night Drew slept well, initially. The stress of having to look after John had been lifted from his shoulders. Though in reality, over the last week or so, John had become a worthy adult.

What woke up Drew at 3 am he did not know, but a word swirled in his mind. It was elusive. It flitted across his consciousness, like a bat. Frustratingly, Drew could not quite grasp it. It annoyed him and he would not drift off to sleep until he sorted it out.

Betrayal!

Finally, this was the word which had bugged Drew.

What a fool I have been to trust Peter bloody Dickinson! thought Drew. From the bomb blast incident in Belfast, he had been conned by his friend, his buddy, his oppo - a comrade who he would have killed, or died, for. It had all been based on a barefaced lie.

You idiot! Drew chastised himself. To add insult to injury, he had let himself be duped for a second time by protecting John de Witt.

To make matters even worse, Drew ignored the warning signs from the kidnapping in the Caribbean. The fact that Peter had masterminded the whole incident was blindingly obvious. There were more red flags than on Tiananmen Square, for heaven's sake! he berated himself.

Drew ground his teeth as he wallowed in recrimination and self-pity. Tomorrow and tomorrow and tomorrow, thought Drew, reciting a vaguely remembered line from Shakespeare's Macbeth. Drew's life could be a torment of endless,

meaningless days until death came as a blessed relief.
　　Sleep...

25. SAHAGÚN TO EL BURGO RANERO

<u>361 km to Santiago de Compostela.</u>

The beeping came from a high-tech monitor, measuring Drew's health condition. He had been transferred during the night to the neuro-surgical ward at a prestigious university hospital. His brain injury was catastrophic and he visualised the surgical team already preparing for an emergency operation.

Coming out of his dream, Drew opened his eyes expecting to see an array of medical equipment, not the underside of the bunk bed above him. He was still in the *albergue*, not the intensive care ward. The beeping sound he heard was a wake-up alarm on a phone in the dormitory.

Drew remembered the conflict in his mind. Sadness that Dixie had taken his life. Coupled with a sense of resentment that he had been deceived by him. The shocking video he watched. A half-remembered thought about tomorrow, in his dreams.

What was that about 'Tomorrow' Drew pondered.

Ah yes, probably 'Tomorrow is another day.' The phrase, filled with positivity and promise, repeated by Scarlett O'Hara in Gone with the Wind. That must have been it, he thought to himself with a smile.

With that in mind, Drew launched into his morning routine with renewed vigour. It was nearing 7 am and he had a long way to go to El Burgo Ranero.

◆ ◆ ◆

The Way left Sahagún through a park and alongside a main road. It was not long before Drew caught up with two familiar *peregrinas*, Grace and Kym.

Grace was wearing earbuds and was singing aloud, "Whoa, we're halfway there! Whoa oh, livin' on a prayer!"

She stopped abruptly when she noticed Drew had joined them and laughed with embarrassment.

"Don't stop on my account. I like a bit of Bon Jovi in the morning. Hope you'll sing The Final Countdown when you get to Lavacolla," said Drew, happy to have the company.

"Yes classic by Joey Tempest, I think. Anyway I imagined you'd take a lie-in and collect yourself half a *compostela*," said Kym, as she went on to explain that Sahagún was a village where you could pick up a certificate to confirm you had completed half of the *Camino Frances.*

"Had heard that, but I didn't fancy hanging around until ten o'clock. Wanted to get going, clear my head," said Drew.

"Speaking of which. How is your poor old head today?" asked Kym.

"My noggin is fine," said Drew, "but yesterday I heard that a friend had taken his life. So I do apologise if I'm a bit down in the dumps today."

Kym had been involved in grief counselling as a nurse and allowed Drew to open up about his feelings as they walked along. Grace pushed on ahead, singing her heart out.

Drew explained that his friend's life had been built on a pack of lies and it had all come tumbling down.

"I don't know how he ended his life, but I can't stop imagining him all alone and desperately sad at the end," Drew confessed with a sigh.

"I would think he was content," said Kym.

Drew was incredulous, "What?"

"Oh yes. In my experience people can become overloaded with stressors. So much so that it becomes utterly unbearable. So your friend identified a way out to end it all. At that point virtually nothing could probably alter his plan. In fact, I bet he was in a state of contentment at the end, he had found his way out of the situation. So don't be sad, at the end of his life he wasn't unhappy."

Drew discussed this further with Kym and

gradually felt a sense of comfort about Dixie's last moments. He was even able to recount a story about his friend in happier times when they were stationed in Germany.

"I had just joined the battalion in Detmold, straight from our recruit training depot at Bassingbourn when I met Dixie," said Drew. "He was my section commander and had just turned twenty-one."

"Let me guess," said Kym. "Alcohol was involved."

Drew laughed and said that Dixie, and several others, got intoxicated in the barracks before they went to the local disco. Because they were so uproariously drunk the bouncers would not let them in, so they slipped in through the backdoor past the DJ.

"Dixie was thrown out by the bouncers and for some unaccountable reason he decided to cool off in the local duck pond," explained Drew.

"Well of course he would," said Kym, suspecting that there was even more to this story.

"On leaving the pond, and not wishing to get hypothermia, Dixie stripped off. Then he had the bright idea of returning to the disco. He used the backdoor again, passed the DJ and started strutting his stuff on the dancefloor completely naked."

"Upholding the finest traditions of Her Majesty's armed forces," said Kym. "Not."

The alcohol finally took its toll and Drew saw

Dixie collapse. "Well we couldn't just leave our comrade behind, so a couple of us grabbed Dixie's feet and we dragged him out to the front door. The bouncers were incandescent with rage. So Dixie was left in the foyer spreadeagled, as naked as the day he was born, and we ran for it," said Drew.

Both Drew and Kym were helpless with laughter.

The route was a pleasant mixture of walking alongside a road and going through farmland. Drew thought that the company was very pleasant too. It had briefly distracted him from thinking about John de Witt. Drew imagined John being whisked away to Madrid airport by Isabella and her idiot sidekick, Juan, for the flight to Johannesburg. Undoubtedly a first class seat, paid for by his father, awaited. He visualised John being served a glass of champagne as the cabin crew asked him how he would like his steak cooking.

Kym asked Drew about his service in the army. They compared notes on their careers and came to the conclusion that there was an affinity between nurses and soldiers. Both knew that the thread of life was very thin indeed and you only live once.

After nearly two hours the pilgrims came to a picnic area. Grace and Kym were planning on a long break, Drew decided to carry on.

"It's been delightful to walk with you, but I need to think a few things through," said Drew.

"Don't think too hard with that battered old brain of yours," advised Grace.

❖ ❖ ❖

Drew walked along the monotonous track.

Crunch, crunch, crunch went his boots on the gravel path. Tap, tap, tap went his trekking pole as it hit the ground. Slosh, slosh, slosh went the liquid in his water bottle. Creak, creak, creak went his rucksack shoulder straps. And on he went. On his own.

He reviewed the last few weeks since he met Dixie in the Minerva pub in Plymouth. Drew and John had dealt with trauma, unwanted romantic overtures, an attempted mugging, the paparazzi and a psychopathic stalker.

On the flip side he mentally kicked himself for allowing himself to get drugged. He smiled at the thought of him, a man in his sixties, brawling with Juan.

The self-recrimination about being duped by Peter Dickinson was hard to bear. As was the fact that he took his own life.

Look on the bright side, thought Drew. John was doing well. Very well actually. From a spoiled brat to a born again good guy.

❖ ❖ ❖

While Drew was wrapped up in his own thoughts, he was oblivious to the fact that he was being followed.

Since leaving Sahagún two watchers had been

trailing him. They kept their distance. Usually a few hundred metres behind. With his distinctive day-glow yellow patch on his rucksack, Drew was easy to keep under observation. The watchers were strong, fit and could easily keep pace with their quarry.

The watchers waited for the right moment to strike. They were patient. Time was on their side.

◆ ◆ ◆

Bercianos del Real Camino was a great place for a coffee and, maybe something a little stronger, Drew thought. At the Hostal Rivero, Drew ordered his usual coffee and a shot glass of brandy, *café cortado y chupito*.

Drew removed his rucksack and kicked off his boots. He had now accepted that he was relieved of the responsibility of minding John. Drew was now on his own. He started drinking his coffee and thought about how strong the sweet local brandy would taste.

One thing that had changed, while walking with John, was his practice of leaving his phone on. He was about to switch it off when it rang. The caller was John.

"Hey Drew, I didn't get a chance to say goodbye. I heard about Pete. I'm really sorry man," said John.

"Hi John," said Drew, delighted to hear from him. "Thanks. Sorry for what?"

"Well that Pete is dead and that he lied about saving your life when you were soldiers."

"Yeah. It's all very sad," Drew said.

"Pete was shown the Belfast video in that meeting he had with the head of HR," said John.

Drew changed the subject, "Hey, I'm so glad you're okay. Hope you implement your changes in the company when you get back home."

"Oh another thing. Xavier found out that Pete had pocketed the ransom money from my kidnap. We can guess who the 'fourth man' was now I suppose. In a way I think we have both been screwed over by Pete."

"We figured out that he was not to be trusted. So it is no real surprise."

"But hey man, we had a good time on the *Camino*. You taught me stuff. Also I learnt a lot about myself. I still have my demons, but I'm doing okay. What are you doing?"

"Oh, same old. In a café on my way to El Burgo Ranero," said Drew, gripping the brandy shot glass to warm its contents.

"You're not going to drink that brandy alone are you?" said John.

Drew spun around and saw John walk through the front door of the café, with an ear to ear grin, still holding his phone.

"Hey! How did you know I'd be here?" said Drew, giving John a hug.

"I just had to follow you. You are a man of regular habits. Tailed you from Sahagún. This is the first café so I reckoned you'd stop here. You taught me well, man."

"Thought you were heading back home though," said Drew, glad to be given the chance to say farewell in person with John.

"So did everyone else," said John, laughing, "My dad is furious, as expected. I've finished with the local security team. By the way, Juan reckons he kicked your arse!"

"Yes he bloody did!" said Drew, laughing. "He sucker punched me in the guts and thumped me in the head. I went down like a sack of spuds. Most unedifying, but I think I deserved it for breaking that bastard's nose. So are you heading off to Joburg now?"

"Not just yet... I reckon life can wait a couple of weeks until I get to Santiago," said John. "Would you mind if I tagged along with you?"

"Only if you must," said Drew, smiling at the fine young man John had become.

Drew put his boots back on and his rucksack.

"Remember to tighten the laces to stop them rubbing your heels," advised John. Drew just smiled at him.

"Let's walk," John said as they left the café.

A pilgrim with a happy smile and a NY Yankees baseball cap was waiting outside the café at a table.

Drew looked at John quizzically.

"Oh yeah, I forgot to say, Ellen's with me. She's coming too," said John.

EPILOGUE: LAVACOLLA TO SANTIAGO

<u>10 km to Santiago de Compostela.</u>

"Did ya know that Lavacolla actually means 'douche yer butt?'" said Ellen, reading a random fact from her phone. John was mid-gulp and spluttered coffee over the kitchen table in the *albergue.*

"Do you mind? I'm having my brekkie," said Drew as he chewed on a chocolate granola bar, with somewhat reduced enthusiasm.

The three pilgrims had registered on the Santiago Pilgrim Office website online and had screenshots of their QR codes on their phones. They were ready to finish their *Camino*.

"So Drew, what's your plan after you get to Santiago?" asked Ellen.

"Go home for a long lie down in a dark room," said Drew, grinning.

"And after that?" asked John.

"Well a friend of mine has raved about this route called the *Camino de Madrid*. Once my old feet have recovered from this adventure, I will start planning to do that one."

"Sounds *lekker.* I will look into-" John started to say, before Drew put up his hand to stop him in his tracks.

"Don't take this the wrong way, John, but this *Camino* has been quite enough excitement for this *Ouballie.* You are not invited to join me again. Ever," Drew said, smiling.

"Okay, I take the hint I'm not welcome Drew. And so, for the very last time," said John. "Let's walk."

◆ ◆ ◆

With an old familiarity the three pilgrims put on their rucksacks and left the *albergue* with just 10 kilometres to go to Santiago de Compostela, their physical journey's end.

They crossed the main road, which was busy with fast moving airport traffic. The Way led down a rural track and they almost missed the right turn along the edge of a field. At a campsite along The Way they stopped to get their first of the two stamps in their *credentials* for the day, plus three *café cortados* and *Neapolitanas.*

Before they knew it the Cathedral towers of Santiago were in view from Monte do Gozo. Soon they walked through the outskirts of the city with massive smiles, like millions of pilgrims before them. As they entered the centre they saw other pilgrims with cardboard tubes, bought from the pilgrim office, containing their priceless *compostelas.* There was a mix of locals, tourists, beggars and pilgrims crowding the maze of streets between the many big honey-coloured stone buildings.

Using the QR codes on their phones they were processed efficiently through the pilgrim office and were issued their *compostelas* and distance certificates. They shopped for other trinkets in the gift shop before moving to the Praza do Obradoiro in front of the Cathedral for photographs and to greet other pilgrims they knew, the two Frenchmen, Lena the Japanese woman, Tom from Chicago, Frank the New Yorker, Peter from New South Wales and last, but by no means least, Linton.

After a while they went to collect John's holdall containing his excess stuff, including his beloved Springboks cap, from *Casa Ivar.* Their empty stomachs led them across the street to a caféteria, for a late breakfast with the locals.

When they were replete with eggs and bacon the trio went to Pilgrim House, which claims it is, 'everything you could want from a great *albergue*, apart from a bed.'

As they were relaxing and chatting with one of the hosts, a woman arrived who Drew recognised immediately.

"Hello there Rocky. Been in any fights lately?" said Kym, miming a boxer with her fists jabbing the air.

"Hiya Kym. I've been very well behaved

recently. For once," said Drew, unable to hide his delight at seeing her again.

"Glad to hear it," said Kym fixing Drew with a long stare with her piercing blue eyes. "A hard man's good to find."

"Don't you mean..." Drew started to correct Kym, but her saucy smile was all the understanding he needed.

"I meant to thank you for helping me out after my last fight," said Drew.

"Don't take it up professionally. If you fell out of a boat you couldn't hit water," she said laughing. "Next time you need some TLC, reach out and get in touch with me." Kym took Drew's hand and slowly wrote her phone number on his palm.

Leaving their rucksacks in Pilgrim House the trio set off towards the Cathedral, although Drew would have enjoyed staying behind just a little bit longer.

❖ ❖ ❖

In the Cathedral they climbed the stairs behind the statue of Saint James. Drew embraced the apostle and prayed for a policewoman who once saved his life.

Blinking back tears, he walked down the stairs into the crypt, under the altar, to view the place where the remains of Saint James rested. Drew knelt and he thought about what the *Camino* had been all about. The hardship, danger, adventure, fraternity, introspection and laughter.

John planned to attend the pilgrim mass the following day as he had paid for the gigantic incense burner, the *botafumeiro,* to be in full swing.

❖ ❖ ❖

After collecting their rucksacks from Pilgrim House, they returned to the Praza do Obradoiro. The time had come for Drew to say goodbye to John and Ellen.

"I've got a train to catch," said Drew.

"I've heard that the drivers don't wait," said John as he handed Drew a pilgrim office carrier bag. "A couple of trinkets for the journey from me. And my dad."

"Oh that's nice, you really didn't have to," Drew said, as John threw his arms around him in a bear hug.

"This *Camino* has changed my life. There was no way I could have done it without you, man."

"It has also changed my life too John," said Drew, "and there was definitely no way I could have done it without you."

John put on a NY Yankees baseball cap as Ellen put on a Springboks cap. They waved Drew goodbye and walked into the *Parador* hotel, hand in hand.

Drew walked down the hill towards the railway station. He smiled as he looked into the carrier bag at a sun-bleached, battered beige baseball cap with a yellow arrow and a thick envelope from a grateful father, containing a 'few quid'.

The hardest part of Drew's *Camino* now lay ahead. Somehow, he needed to meet the family of a woman who gave her young life for his, one wet afternoon in Belfast many years ago.

CAMINO VETERAN
PROLOGUE: MOSCOW
& PARIS

This year's Victory Day parade in Moscow would be unforgettable.

The annual celebration in May of the Soviet forces' victory over Nazi Germany in the Second World War started, as usual, with a march-past of thousands of men and women from the armed forces of the Russian Federation. The massed bands played as the leaden skies of the capital produced a flurry of snow. The president and his entourage of top military leaders, and aged war veterans, looked on proudly from their VIP grandstand.

Military analysts and commentators around the world watched the live images avidly to scrutinise the Red Army's latest display of military hardware.

◆ ◆ ◆

In the Paris headquarters of the Direction

Générale de la Sécurité Extérieure (DGSE) the CEO received a cryptic text message on her personal phone, '*Regardez le lanceur de missiles nucléaires à Moscou. Vous êtes les bienvenus. L'administrateur.*' (Look at the nuclear missile launcher in Moscow. You are welcome. The administrator). Somewhat bemused, she switched on the TV coverage from Red Square.

◆ ◆ ◆

A solitary World War Two era Soviet T34 tank clattered along Red Square, trailing a cloud of exhaust fumes. In place of the usual display of the latest T90 and the futuristic T14 *Armata* tanks, there followed rows of *Tigr* 4×4 all-purpose wheeled armoured vehicles. Commentators would be having a field day reporting on the absence of main battle tanks on parade.

Next came the 47 tonne intercontinental ballistic missile, the *Topol-M*, on its massive 16-wheel transporter. The 22 metre long missile could carry a 800 kiloton nuclear warhead.

Interesting, thought the French CEO, a lot of lightly armoured wheeled vehicles followed by a thumping great nuke. What is the Russian President trying to say? Her analytical mind mused about US President Theodore Roosevelt's policy of, 'Speak softly and carry a big stick,' when it happened.

The missile launcher stopped abruptly right

in front of the VIP stand. The circuitry of the automatic onboard fire extinguisher triggered and a great cloud of CO_2 billowed from the vehicle.

In Paris, the CEO held her breath, before muttering, "*Sacre bleu!*"

The driver and commander of the missile transporter were dumbfounded. It was as if all of their onboard electronic systems had crashed simultaneously. They knew that they were not in any imminent danger as the missile container they carried on top of their vehicle was empty. Their real *Topol-M* missile was safely stored in its bunker back at base. There was no way any sane person would bring a live nuclear missile onto the parade. However, the spectators, and most of the massed ranks of service personnel, were unaware of this. What they saw was a huge nuclear missile carrier swathed in smoke; what they did was - run.

As thousands of *Muscovites* and soldiers sprinted for their lives, security personnel evacuated the grandstand and the President was bundled unceremoniously into his protected vehicle.

Inside the missile transporter the crew were unaware of the pandemonium which their vehicle had caused due to all of the smoke. On the bright side, their engine management unit had automatically rebooted itself and the vehicle dashboard had come back to life. With much relief, the driver managed to restart the engine and drove forwards out of the smoke screen, to see a state of utter chaos.

Although some units were still standing rigidly to attention, most had fled, including the band who had discarded their instruments in the process. Several of the *Tigr* vehicles had collided with each other as they tried to get as far away as possible, as quickly as possible. It was mayhem.

The Presidential armoured limousine sped off towards the Kremlin. Inside the vehicle the air was filled with expletives and an order to find out who the hell had caused the, 'кучка дерьма' (clusterfuck).

◆ ◆ ◆

Back in the 20th *arrondissement* in Paris, the CEO called a snap meeting of her 'inner circle' to tell them that one of their former technical officers, codename *L'administrateur*, probably caused the fiasco in Moscow.

As the attendees took their seats in her office she wondered why this 'problem child' still polluted the universe with his very existence.

She recalled the fateful words of the English King Henry II which led to the murder of Thomas Becket in Canterbury, 'Will no one rid me of this turbulent priest!'

CAMINO VETERAN

Cloak-and-dagger on the *Camino de Madrid*

Codename Veteran was unique. His legendary ability to bypass security on electronic systems was second to none. He could paralyse a vehicle, train, ship, aircraft or even a country's entire vital infrastructure.

Veteran's disillusionment with the secret intelligence community made him a loose cannon. MI6 decided to groom this maverick genius and recruit him to be the country's best cyber security asset, before the competition could use him against the UK. Time was running out.

MI6 had one opportunity to cultivate Veteran as he walked the *Camino de Madrid* and, by chance, they had the ideal man to do it - Drew Mallam. The stakes could not have been higher.

As Veteran trekked from Madrid along the pilgrimage route towards Santiago de Compostela Drew attempted to acquire him for MI6, but could he do this before the competition?

amazon.com/author/mikemcbride

ACKNOWLEDGEMENTS

To my family and friends for your unwavering support.

My profound thanks go to Martin, Samantha and Jim for proofreading. I take full responsibility for any errors.

To Warren Kramer, an amazing graphic designer, thank you for staying the course with me and creating yet another great cover.

To all fellow pilgrims, hospitaleros/as, and the locals I have met somewhere along The Way - you have been my inspiration.

For those men and women in the real close protection world who earn their living by getting in harm's way for us - thank you.

COPYRIGHT © MIKE MCBRIDE, 2024

This book is sold subject to the condition that it shall not, by way of trade or otherwise, be lent, resold, hired out, or otherwise circulated without the author's prior consent in any form of binding or cover other than that in which it is published and without a similar condition including this condition being imposed on the subsequent publisher.

The moral right of Mike McBride has been asserted.

This is a work of fiction. Unless otherwise indicated, all the names, characters, businesses, places, events and incidents in this book are either the product of the author's imagination or used in a fictitious manner. Any resemblance to actual persons, living or dead, or actual events is purely coincidental.

In particular, the De Witt company is a product of the author's imagination and should not be associated with any company, corporation or business of a similar name.

BOOKS BY THIS AUTHOR

<u>Non-fiction</u>

    Street Survival Skills
    Crime Patrol
    UK Police Guide
    European Police Firearms
    Jane's Police and Homeland Security Equipment
    Last Stand at Zandvoorde 1914

<u>Fiction</u>

 <u>Drew Mallam series:</u>

  Camino Calling

  Camino Bodyguard

  Camino Veteran

 <u>Frankie de la Fonte series:</u>

  Camino Crossroads

  Camino Spirit

  amazon.com/author/mikemcbride

Printed in Great Britain
by Amazon